The Misdemeanours of Tinder

The Misdemeanours of Tinder

The memoirs of a menopausal serial dater

Maria R. Peter

I dedicate this book to all the wonderful characters we meet during our online dating journeys. To all that, take part. I hope you find what you are looking for, be that love or fun.

She is fire and ice
Soft but strong
She is a total badass
With a good heart

Why Tinder?

Single too long, loneliness as a single mum, hopeful, belief in love and that my Mr Right could be just one swipe right away. To create a Tinder profile was not a simple decision. Mulling over it for a while before I took that definite step. I had been single for two years, watching my friends having relative success on the infamous dating app. I am ok looking, doing all right for my age. My hair is all my own, not grey, and still in possession of my teeth. Boobs and bum still standing. Upon reflection, I can guarantee this wasn't my brightest idea. I was still finding my path in the world after my last relationship. I felt I had lost my identity. The relationship lasted 13 years, and it was not the healthiest. I lost myself; I was subject to his cruel jibes and temper. His control over me was absolute.

When I met him, it was just me and my son, also with a career I had dreamt of since being a little girl, working with the rich and famous, travelling the globe. Childhood dreams became my reality. The feel of dance shoes on my feet. All I needed was a partner to share my world with. Go on adventures and be with my best mate. I am the monogamous type, loyal to my detriment sometimes. But that New Year's Eve, when I caught his eye from the other side of the club, instantly smitten. One bottle of Bacardi later and he was mine.

My mind convincing itself that I have found the one! The search is over. Never again would I have another man. We had an idyllic first year. Others might call it an extended honeymoon period. Falling pregnant before the year was out. The flaws in our relationship made an appearance. He turned into a controlling human being, constantly putting me down, making me lose any faith I had myself. Doubts creeped in and I no longer thought of myself as a vibrant, intelligent, successful, sexy woman. I now thought I was fat, ugly, and stupid. The birth of our daughter brought a fleeting relief. Intense jibes and digs started. Dents to my confidence and self-belief, I never seemed to get anything right. Deterioration to my self-esteem was slow but steady.

Trapped in a relationship that supplies no happiness to either of us. We did what any couple would do. We had another baby! The trauma of our beautiful boy, diagnosed with autism, was just one step too far for the survival of our relationship. Left to deal with all the appointments. All the heartbreak on my own. There was no going back. We deteriorated at breakneck speed. Independence and freedom were something I sought. Learnt to drive. Got a job. Rediscovery of my true self. I found the strength to go alone. The world was my oyster!

I might have found my freedom, but I soon discovered I was extremely shy and had a lack of confidence. Barely recognising this human staring back at me in the mirror. I reconnected with the friends I had lost during my time with him. Without their support, the metaphorical prison built to keep me would have become forever.

Was I ready? Was I healed? We all know the answer to that! No! Still owning an innocence and naivete when I embarked on my Tinder journey. A woman of the world, I led myself to believe that I had a good understanding of men. I worked with guys throughout my career and had plenty of male friends. How wrong was I?

After much encouragement, I decided tonight was the night to start. I got myself together, shower, washed the mop, a large glass of wine and I was ready. It was now or never! The time was right! Time set aside building a profile, choosing the pictures, thinking of the right words to use for the best description of myself.

Tinder, show me my Mr Right!

Maria R Peter

1.... 2.... 3... and swipe!

The serial swiper!

Now I am ready, I am swiping, and the matches are happening! I will be in a relationship before you know it. Full of hope that he is there in his living room, waiting for my profile to appear before him. The promise of desire and the rest will be history. That's how it works, right? WRONG!
Welcome to the arena of the serial swiper!

I was so new to this; You matched, you chat and get to know each other. At this stage, I am still optimistic. Just to point out that my optimism never waned until I reached the point of writing this journal. I have told many of my friends on our girls' nights over a bottle of wine, my trials, and tribulations. Mostly to laughter and jaws to the floor, exclamations of disbelief!

So, the first match is in, they just kept coming. I am going to be truthful; I felt validated! I am attractive. Men do want to know me. They made me to believe I was not worthy of love. One hundred and twenty matches in one night! I had arrived! I know what you are thinking. You can't get that many! I had become a serial swiper overnight without even realising I was doing it. I was so excited! Like a kid in the candy store. All these men paraded in front of me, all looking like potential possibilities for my future. A new addiction begins. The same highs and lows of a mind-bending drug.

The opening line was something I had to think about. I didn't know the protocol. I like to be approached in a gentlemanly fashion. This was completely unfamiliar territory for me. I wanted to show them I was more than just a picture, that there were plenty of sides of me. I wanted to show my humour and my smiles. My personality! I don't know how to do it with a text message. I bet you are all dying to know what that line was?

WHAT WAS YOUR FAVOURITE FLAVOUR FROM THE ALPINE POP MAN?

Now why would I ask this? I wanted to stand out. I wanted to know that the person I was talking to was the age they said they were and would understand my working-class background. And to evoke a childhood memory and a conversation starter.

Lo-and-behold it worked! The responses were coming back. More than I could cope with, so the process of elimination started. Do not roll your eyes, we all do it! Most were of the laughing emoji, some saying that was the best line they had ever received on Tinder. Others just simply reply. "Funny, but can I fuck you?" Charming! DELETE!

There was still hope. I had many conversations over that week. The figure had gone from one hundred and twenty down to four. I was getting along with them fine. It felt like I cheated on them all. Connections were happening. What did I do? I continued to keep swiping. Right now, I hold my head in my hands. I just was not ready to commit to an actual date at that moment, even though I had the request of my company. The menu had too much choice. No one stood out yet. I asked myself several times, why if the conversation was flowing and we are getting along, some of them disappear, then realisation dawned! I was doing the same thing! It was simply becoming chatting and NEXT! If this happens to you, don't worry, you have done the same thing.

But finally, one stuck, and the first date was about to happen. This is it. I can stop looking! Or so I thought.!

Mr Control Freak

I must have been on dates during my time on Tinder? Yes. Quite a few. Some good, some bad, some just downright unbelievable. So, let me take you on a journey through the calamity of my dating life. There are too many dates to mention. It's exhausting! But there were ones that made good dinner party or girls' nights tales with many standout moments. That should always be a warning. A huge red flag to alert me to the outcomes of each. All the singletons can identify with one chapter in this book.

I am going to start with my very first Tinder date! How excited was I? Meet Mr Control Freak. So, it happened. I had agreed to meet someone. We had been chatting for a couple of weeks and we got along, and the conversation was flowing. He was a pilot out of the country and would return the next day. But lived about 20 mins away from me. I waited patiently for him to ask me. Then the text come through. "Do you fancy a coffee sometime? I would love to meet you in person. " So, was this it? Was I about to meet my destiny?

We arranged a date at a lovely little restaurant and bar in the posh part of town. Afternoon coffee date. What could go wrong? I had 2 days to prepare. It was the middle of summer, and the sun was blazing down, and I couldn't just turn up in my usual summer staple of cut-off jeans and vest top and maybe a pair of sandals if you were lucky. First, looking in the mirror, and second my wardrobe, I realised how much I had let myself go. My confidence just took a massive nosedive. In a moment of trying to convince myself I was financially better off than I was, I checked the bank account. Not much going on there. Do I go for a splurge on the credit card or opt for Primark? I opted for latter, as I did not want to get carried off with myself.

I was in decent shape and the legs were looking slim and tanned, so I opted for a lovely pair of cobalt blue tailored shorts, with a little vest top and biker jacket. Now for a pair of heels. I wanted my short legs to give the impression of a youthful gazelle.

The next morning, I woke to a text from Mr Control Freak, "Morning gorgeous, Sorry I didn't text yesterday. It was late when I got home and went straight to bed. I can't wait to see you later," In my hopeful mind, my Tinder days were over before they had begun. Will I feel attracted to him? I prayed!

I spent the entire morning in preparation. Legs shaved, tan topped up, rat tails painfully extracted from my mane after it had been in a bun for days. Now for make-up! Then the realisation dawned. I don't own any! Panic stations! An hour out shopping for products I had no clue how to use. When did make-up get so complicated?

Finally, I was ready. Smooth legs, smooth hair, and passable make-up. If I kept my hair down, no one would see the foundations lines as I had bought the wrong colour. The nerves were kicking in, ready to abandon the mission. What if he thought I was ugly, stupid, fat, not likeable? All those doubts from my last relationship kicked in. On text I was coming across as a strong, confident woman, but was I really? Was he going to get the woman he was expecting? Quick phone call to the girls and suddenly I was pulling into the car park of our chosen venue. Was I early? Has he stood me up? Or was I late? My mind was all over the place and I couldn't think straight.

I took a deep breath and walked into the restaurant, and there he was. Sat at the bar, patiently waiting for me. He turned around with a huge smile and I felt a wave of relief. He was more handsome than his pictures. His eyes were of the most intense grey. He fascinated me. Staring at him the way one would watch the chimpanzees in the zoo, watching his every movement. Then he stood up. It wasn't his height; I like little men. He was five foot eight; it was his attire. Flares with heavily polished cowboy boots and unbuttoned shirt down to his naval. Now I know I shouldn't be judgemental, but you need a common ground on style. Visions of mirrored ceilings in his apartment were popping into my head. This was a 53-year-old playboy going through a midlife crisis. Stay positive, do not judge too quickly. My head could not make its mind up, spinning from all the options. Do I make a run for it or just enjoy the company? I chose to stay, and I am glad I did. It opened my eyes to the magical world of Tinder dating.

He was so handsome and there was a physical spark between us, but I just kept focusing on the boots. I could not help myself. I smirked and laughed at his jokes. He was a funny guy, and the conversation was interesting. It was going well. What cowboy boots? Forgotten, pushed to the deep recesses of my mind. If that were all I could find wrong with the guy, then surely, we were onto a winner.

Remember, by this point, we had talked about the possibility of a second date, closing the Tinder accounts, see where it went. Then it came. The truth about this guy. The control freak was about to rear its ugly head. He reached into his pocket, me still in my naïve mind was thinking he was about to show me something. Out came the piece of A4 paper with a list on it. Why would he want to show me his Waitrose shopping list? This was his grocery store of choice. No doubt about it.

He handed me the list, and I took it anxiously. What could this be? Then the bomb dropped, as did my jaw. The list was his requirements of what he expects from his girlfriend. I could not believe what I was reading and for the guy to be upfront about this. I had lived with a control freak for years, but this was on a different level.

As a pilot, he was only home for three days a week. He expected me to be at his apartment waiting for him, dressed in heels and lingerie only. This would be the only attire I would need for the time I was with him. I was to cook and clean for him in this state of dress and be sexually available to him upon his request. He would expect me to always appear perfect, with hair, nails and make-up done while I was with him

My indignation was rising, but I was also seeing the funny side. The temptation to entertain myself was too much. If you ask any of my friends, this is a flying red rag to a bull in the wind-up stakes. I pretended to go along with his outrageous demand, asking many questions.

"Do I have to wear my heels at the gym?"

"What about my kids?"

"Did he have enough bedrooms for us all?"

"Why didn't I just move in as it would be easier, then I would always be available to him whenever he came home?"

"Do I wear lingerie at the office, or do I just give up work and stay at his home for his leisure?"

These questions were all answered solemnly and seriously. What had happened to the man on the other end of the phone? Where was the sense of humour I had grown to like? I was so disheartened. No one was ever going to control me unless it's control I had asked for!

As he walked me to my car, I was silently on my phone blocking him!

Mr Control Freak says...

I am exhausted. Long haul flying is taking its toll on me. Away from home for days at a time. I love my job. I get to travel the world and spend time with air stewards. What man wouldn't want that? Back from the Bahamas and a few days on a yacht to fill my days, cocktails, sun, beaches, while waiting to fly back. As I enter my apartment, the silence hits me with deafening aplomb. If only I had that one special woman to greet with me with the smells of my favourite meal and a glass of red. Standing in my kitchen in her lingerie, ready to serve me.

A few swipes on Tinder before I hit the shower. I've not been very successful of late. I have removed the picture showing me standing in front of a Boeing 787 in my pilot uniform. Since then, my matches have decreased. But I don't want any gold diggers. I want a good standard woman! Women these days seem to want it all. Why? When I could support all their needs. If only they would adhere to my rules. They could have a lifestyle of which they have always dreamed.

I need a woman who takes care of herself but is not too sassy or feisty. It may be a fantasy, but I'm not prepared to lower my standards. Even better if they come with a good level of vulnerability. Easier to bring her round to my way of thinking.

The warmth of the shower leaving my skin with a pink glow. Mixing with the steam is the woodiness of my Tom Ford body wash, tingling all my senses.

As my hands reach for my cock, soapy, smooth strokes, I imagine my dream woman in my favourite La Perla lingerie and Christian Louboutin heels, on her knees, taking me in her warm wet mouth, bringing me to climax. A sharp whistle from my phone brings me back to my senses. I have a match!

Not bad! Good body, nice arse, deep brown eyes. A bit of a tan on her. Is she the one that will bend to my wishes? I hope she is not one of those girls that knows how to dress to hide her flaws. Can't stand a mum tum! I wonder what she looks like in just her knickers, stocking, and heels? Let's message and find out!

After realising she is new to the dating game, coming across with an innocence and I could guarantee she is vulnerable, but laid back and open-minded. She could be the one accepting my views and me! Impressed by my career and worldly ways, I asked her for coffee. Why is she making me wait for her answer? It's been 10 mins. That's not a good start for her. She has a lot of work to do, but I think she is trainable.

"I would love a coffee. Let me know when you are free?"

Finally, a response. We agree to me to meet a lovely restaurant, near to my house. Expensive, tiny plates, but impressive. She better appreciate the effort I am going to make.

I've got the perfect outfit for this rendezvous. The cowboy boots never fail. Purchased while on a break from work in Phoenix, Arizona. Black leather with a white cotton embroidery in a western style, blue jeans with a belt to match the boots. White shirt with buttons casually left undone. A splash of Tom ford aftershave to match the body wash. Wallet, keys, and list in the pocket and I start on the five-minute walk to the restaurant.

I've arrived ten minutes early, put her on the backfoot a little, as she will think she has kept me waiting. It's a nice day, but I decide to sit at the bar with my back turned to the door. That way, I can see her enter the room through the mirror and decide if she is worth turning round for. I know the chef, so I can easily make a quick getaway through the kitchen if need be. The creak of the big glass doors alerts me to her arrival, and I glance in the mirrors to check her out.

She actually looks like her pictures. This is novel for a tinder date. Nice legs. She has arrived wearing shorts and heels. She knows her best assets. I sense her looking around to find me. I can feel her approach me.

"Hi there, nice to meet you, finally. "

I turn around and feel the warmth of her bright smile. The dim spotlights, adding to the shine of her dark hair. I guide her over to a table, checking her out from behind. She walks confidently in high heels. I like that! Good start.

"What would you like to drink?"

With not a moment's hesitation, "Soy vanilla latte". She's decisive and knows what she wants. This might be more difficult than I first thought. I needed her to hesitate so I could take charge and order for her. I do not want her putting on extra pounds, so it would be a flat black, low in calories and no fuss or waiting for the bartender to create this frivolous drink. There is a chocolate powder dusting on my hazelnut cappuccino. I'm paying for the extravagance and if she agrees to my terms and conditions, then I will allow her a few.

Placing my hand on the small of her back, I guide her over to a high table and stools. I need to interview her properly on the low sofas just by the window. The leather warmed from the low evening sun. I cannot have her too comfortable yet. As she sits opposite me, she seems fascinated with me. Direct eye contact always held. I wonder if she has spotted the boots. I have had no one remark on them, so I am presuming they are a winner with the ladies. To be fair, she is stunning to look at, conversation flowing and plenty of laughter. I imagine her naked, bent over my dining table. Feel the corners of my mouth turn up into a flirty smirk. Responding with a smile and throaty, nervous laughter, she looks at me through her eyelashes. She wants me. I can feel it in my pants. That familiar stirring and strain against my jeans. She is a demure flirt, but I need to talk to her about sorting out her make-up application, which is a discussion for the second date. It's best not to rush these things.

"Why have you been single so long?"

"I had a traumatic time with my last relationship and needed time to heal before I started something new. But I do not really want to talk about it now. I'd rather be getting to know you." She speaks with a soft lilt to her voice. I can't quite catch her accent, but it's not local in Manchester.

She has the right amount of vulnerability I need to mould her into the woman I need her to be. As I reach for the list in my back pocket of my jeans, I inhale sharply as I see the look of confusion flashing across her face before she righted herself. I just hand her the list without words. She looks more attractive with puzzlement in her eyes, unable to can't hide her emotions, which is a good thing, all expression disappears as she absorbs the information in front of her. The paper is smooth with her between her fingers. Almost caressing, revelling in the luxury against her skin, confirming she is going to love my satin sheets. I imagine her tanned, toned body writhing against the sensuality of the red. If only I had fitted mirrors on the ceiling.

"Do I have to wear my heels at the gym?"

"You can go to the gym on the days I am away flying,"

"What about my kids?"

"They could stay with their father on the days I am away flying,"

"Did he have enough bedrooms for us all?"

"I have two spare rooms, but only in an emergency. If they need to stay with us occasionally, they could stay there as long as they don't make a mess of the apartment." She seems to be keen, asking genuine questions? I knew she was the one.

"Why didn't I just move in as it would be easier, then I would always be available to him whenever he came home?"

"That sounds like a great idea for the future,"

"Do I wear lingerie at the office, or do I just give up work and stay at his home for his leisure?"

"You won't need to work as I will provide for us both,"

For a first date, this has gone well. She asks if she can have a little time to think about it. I need an answer quickly, but I must keep it respectful for now. The walk back to her car, and the mood has lightened. She tells me excitedly about her new Fiat 500 in a cool gunmetal grey. I cannot stop watching her with her animated chatter. Her energy and excitement for the world around her, so addictive.

"Sorry, I just have to answer this text. It's work." Her smile has disappeared as she concentrates on the screen for a moment.

"All done. Thank you for a lovely date. Speak soon," she said as she climbs into her car.

Those legs are legs of dreams, wrapping around my waist. Rushing home, I open my phone and take a gander at her pictures. Yes, she is warming to me.

I open up my WhatsApp. Her picture has disappeared, strange? "Nice to meet you at last. Can't wait to see you again. "
There must be a fault on the phone. Never heard from her again

Mr Ghoster!

The ghoster must be the most confusing character in Tinder. On reflection, I can attribute most to the acts of the serial swiper. But there are those that just stand out with a genuine quality to them. Gold standard ghosts! Occasionally, it has happened to me. It makes you question everything about yourself, especially if you are having a confidence crisis of a day. It always seems to happen on the days you just want to open your best bottle of red from Aldi and not move from under the duvet. But you cannot. The kids are throwing in their demands, the credit card bill is due, and we pile the desk high with uncompleted work, because a liquid lunch with the girls seemed like a clever idea at the time!

That familiar whistle of Tinder alerts you to the fact you have a match. Just the pickup you need as you once again try to keep up with the email thread. Why do I have to read four weeks of drivel to understand what this latest email means? Just say what you mean. Sod it, my future husband is more important to check out! The thread can wait.

As I tentatively check my match, I am holding my breath. Please do not let it be someone who I swiped with my wine goggles on. Please let fate be on my side.

Eureka! A sight to behold!

Think I better read his profile, as who does until you match! I know I am not the only one! As I am taking in the gorgeous man before me, another notification. Yes! Finally, a match and a message. We are on a winner lady! Fasten your seatbelts and enjoy the ride!

He is ten years younger than me and lives twenty- five miles away. I can live with that. What was the point in learning to drive if it did not help me move forwards to the one that could be the one? Chatting away with Mr Ghoster is so easy. We have loads of common interests. He is a drummer in a band that did well for itself. Not going to lie. I googled him. They had piqued my interest. We talked about my past of working within the music industry, how I loved being on the road in younger days, the camaraderie you developed on the tour bus. The smells, the adventures, the creation of a dysfunctional family, the people you met along the way. How hard it was to meet people who could understand the lifestyle and the trust issues your partner could have while you are away gigging. He was also kinda sexy in a neanderthal kind of way. You know the type. They look like they have just walked into the back end of a bus, but somehow still be handsome.

We swapped numbers within a couple of hours, moving to the more comfortable arena of WhatsApp. The thing I liked about this guy is that he never sent me pictures of himself in his underwear, never asked me to send him any. Respectful. We would speak on the phone every night and I felt like we were really getting to know one another.

I used to pull up his pictures and revel in his handsomeness. He was five foot ten that's tall for me, with deep brown eyes and the manly ruggedness to his face. His arms were the type of arms that you knew when they held you, you would feel safe. So physically and mentally, I was all there, already thinking about being in his arms. I was trying my hardest to play it cool. But after three-hour phone calls every night talking about anything and everything, I was all in. I could not wait to meet him. So, when we got round to arranging a date about five weeks later, it felt like the most natural arrangement in the world. The right progression to make.

The day had come. We had spoken earlier in the morning, all was good. Or so I thought. There was no reason not to. If nothing came of it romantically, I thought I had made a friend for life.
A WhatsApp notification came through an hour before we were supposedly meeting. Naively, I thought it was just going to be the standard "looking forward to seeing you" text. OH NO, if only it was. I open the message and what I read left me stunned, open-mouthed and lost for words.

SOMEONES DIED!

This message just shouted at me! I could not believe what I was reading! But that is all it said. No explanation. No, my nan, or my dog has just passed away. Just Someone has died in glaring huge capital letters! Of course, being the empathic person I am, I responded.
"Hey babe, I am so sorry to hear this news. I hope you are ok. I'm here if you need to talk."
That message unread. The silence was so loud you could hear the tumbleweed straining across my room in my draught-proof house. Now, when this happens, the first thing you do is question yourself. What did I do wrong? Did I say something that he

did not like? Did he just decide I was not attractive enough for him? What???? I am so confused.

I tried reaching out to him a few weeks later to see if he was ok, but nothing. I come off Tinder for a while as I was so hurt by this, I just didn't understand what or how it happened. I blamed myself. I know people meet me and think I am super confident, but I'm a sensitive soul, which you only get to find out once you have chipped away at my walls and I let you in.

I can laugh about this now and when I tell this tale, I shout the now infamous text out with volume and drama, so those listening understand how loud those two words came across to me. I am at the point of questioning everything. I do not think ghosts get the impact their behaviour has. All they need to do is just say, Thanks, but no thanks. Might be harsh, but to be dismissed in such a way is cruel. Take note to those of you that engage in this unexplained online dating activity. I am not talking about the people you match with and do not communicate with or do not get past the hello, but those that get you to invest in them mentally and emotionally. Just wrong!

Bye Tinder…. for now, anyway!

Mr Ghoster says...

I shouldn't be doing this, but my marriage is dead in the water. I love my wife, I really do, but I need to feel that thrill of someone new again. The excitement of going to meet them for the first time. Fulfilment of my physical needs. The smells and tastes of a woman. To remember the thrill of abandonment, feeling someone respond to my touch until we can hold back no more. Noisy sex with the lights on. That's what I want and need. I need to feel wanted again. Since the kids come along, it's a rare occasion and then it is in the dark, its silent and over in a couple of minutes because of the paranoia of them walking in and catching us. When I think back to when I was a child, we could not disturb our parents on a Sunday morning. My siblings and I never knew exactly what was going on, now I understand why they did it. They were keeping the magic alive, keeping that connection between themselves. For us, that was no longer there.

Connecting with women on Tinder is easy. Once they realise you are a drummer, they cannot hold themselves back. We meet for coffee, then meet again for no strings attached fun. Why is this so easy? I've met no one I could fall for. There is no way I could fall in love as my wife has my heart.

I see her profile, a very sexy lady. Older than I usually go for, but she looks good for her age. Let's swipe. What's the worst that could happen? Excellent, we have a match! I message straight away. An instant response. I like how this is going. Too many interests in common, but do I tell her about my other half? That is probably going to go down like a lead balloon.

She will have a good understanding of my lifestyle. Few girls truly have what it takes to be with a drummer from a rock band. We gig all over the northwest and I'm hardly home. Wait! Why am I thinking that way? The aim is just to get this fine specimen of female between the sheets. She doesn't really need to know much about me.

We talked every day and when I didn't, I could feel an emptiness inside me. Somehow, she had filled a void in my life. A light had appeared within me. I smiled as she chattered about anything and revelled in her own silliness. It felt so good to laugh again and forget my troubles. Carefree and a sense of living again reignited.

What is wrong with me I hadn't even met the woman yet? For weeks we chatted until I finally plucked up the courage to ask her on a date. With our schedules, we arranged for a week later at a pub in her part of the world. The anticipation of meeting her was too much to bear. My wife was noticing a change in me. Brushing her off with excuses of work and the band going in the right direction. Guilt clouding my expression, I wasn't supposed to be building a relationship with another, but was I falling for this woman? Is it even possible? We had only texted and talked on the phone. I'd never felt her physicality near me, yet I needed to speak with her, hear her voice!

"Just popping out to get some milk and bread for the morning," closing the door behind to get in the car. How long could I stay out without raising suspicion? The night is dark, driving against the glare of the headlights from the odd car. The roads are quiet. I drive slowly to make the most of the time I had. The nearest shop open was a half hour drive. That gave me plenty of time to phone from the car.

"Hi Babe, how's your day been?"

"Hey, you, I've missed you. Today has dragged. I'm so excited about tomorrow. Finally getting to meet you,"

I can hear the excitement in her voice. My heart raced with affection for she holds for me. The warmth and tenderness, speaking to me in a way my wife used to. I miss the woman I married. We were becoming strangers more each day. I made a commitment to love and honour her for the rest of her life. Through the good and the bad. Sleeping with women I had no emotional connection with didn't count. I was becoming invested in this person, so now it was cheating. Taking things to the next level. After chatting for an hour, I return home.

She must have heard my key turn the lock, waiting for me behind the door. There is something wrong? Realisation hit me. I had forgotten to get groceries.

"Where are the milk and bread? Not that we needed any. I've just checked the fridge. Plenty there," as she turned defeated to the kitchen. Hiding her face from me. I had never seen her like this, her face unable to hide the hurt. She knows! What have I done? Unable to get my mouth working properly, tongue sticking to the roof of my dry mouth, trying to think of a lame excuse. What was the point of lying to her? I join her at the table, positioned so she can't see my face, but I can see her pain. With the stabbing in my chest and knots in my stomach, realising I must take whatever is coming.

"I'm sorry," I said, fingering the rim of my glass.

"Sorry for what?" the obvious anger in her voice that she was trying to keep down. "Is it the Tinder profile my best friend has found?"

"Have you met anyone?"

"Are you talking to someone now?"

"Have you slept with another woman?"

"How many are there?"

The questions were quick, leaving no time for a reply. Firing at me with intention and subdued, passive aggressive ferocity. Not knowing how to answer without truly igniting the fire inside of her. In all our years of marriage, I had never seen her lose her temper. I think I was just about to find out! Even my drum kit wouldn't be able to drown out of the sounds in my heart and head. The pounding was inescapable.

As I dared to look up, mascara and tears curdling on her face, cursing the fact that I was in such a bubble I hadn't noticed when entering our family home. I'd not just betrayed her, but also our unit as a family. This needed to be fixed. Could I repair the damage? I see once again the woman I had fallen in love with, and she was hurting because of my actions. Never again could I do this to her and the kids, my selfish behaviour to be brought to a halt.

We retired to bed, hoping the dawn would bring a fresh start. I woke, knowing what I had to do. It would be brutal and cold, but there was no other way. The connection was to be severed. My wife slept peacefully, hugging the pillow and her back to me. My silent phone showing the notification I desperately didn't want to see. It was her, full of hope of the outcome of our meeting today. What to say? There was no way to let her down gently. If she felt a fraction of what I was feeling, this was going to be bad.

"SOMEONES DIED!"

It's done. My wife is the perfect spoon and the only person who can fix my broken heart. She pushes back into me as I feel my erection grow, finding its way towards her sweet spot. Making love to her for the first time in years and all my healing was done.

Mr Catfish!

I've had a break from online dating, but all I am seeing around me is my friends getting into successful relationships. Why can't I have a piece of the action? These men don't know what they are missing!

Friends always trying to fix me up with unsuitable men. The type they wouldn't touch with a barge pole. But I'm desperate in their eyes. I'll be old soon and no one will want me according to them. My standards are too high, I expect too much blah blah blah! The list goes on. So back to my old friend Tinder. I can always rely on them to provide me with virtual company and amusement. What is in store for me now? Even I could not predict this one, but my curiosity got the better of me. I knew I was playing with fire, but I just couldn't help myself.

Happily swiping away, doing a bit of dating window shopping. In front of me, all the potential prospects that could be lucky enough to be my future partner! I came across a profile, in which the beauty displayed in front of me seemed ever so familiar. Was I questioning if it could be him? Why would he be first on Tinder? Second, just down the road in Sheffield? It was only Magic Mike himself, the one and only Channing Tatum. This must be my lucky night!

Before you say it! I know it wasn't Channing, but I had a couple of gins and the thought of the game that was about to play out was too tantalising and intriguing not to swipe right. What tipsy woman wouldn't? Yes, at this point I am rolling my eyes and holding my head in my hands at my sheer stupidity, but I blame it all on the delicious rhubarb gin gifted to me for Christmas, and besides there was nothing I wanted to watch on the TV. I needed entertaining. I was in control of this; I kept telling myself. I knew exactly what I was getting myself into. Or did I?

Fingers numb from texting, we moved quickly onto a phone call. The conversation was full and dynamic. All the while, I know this man is not true. I so wish he could have been. Allowing myself to drift into the fantasy that was being created between us. His deep Yorkshire accent, reminiscent of a hero from a romance novel, driving right into the core of my physical being. I try my hardest not to think of the man behind the voice. Open and honest chatter, going deep into our political and emotional minds. Why am I being so open and honest with this man?

Letting him know my innermost secrets and fears? This is only going to lead to hurt or disaster.

As the words keep tumbling from my mouth, I realise I am using this man as a free therapy session. I had a lot to get off my chest. Telling all the tales from my past, my poor treatment from different men, my vulnerabilities. What harm could it do? I needed to talk to someone, to understand why everything in my life happened and what could I do to change this pattern. I would never meet this man; I knew he was not what or who he was saying. Busy distracted with the conversation, an alert comes through. He has sent me a picture.

"This is me as a body double for Channing!".

The sheer audacity of this man knows no boundaries. To know that he thinks I am taken in by all this charade is a tremendous blow to the ego of my intelligence levels, or he is just getting carried away with his little self. He is believing his own bullshit! My stomach is gnarling with the slow build-up of anger at this man.

"Oops! Sorry, my phone has died. I am going to say goodnight. Nice chatting with you." I brazenly text after slamming my finger onto the end call button. I did not want to hear anymore.

"No problem, we can catch up tomorrow?" he hopefully questions at the same time of sending a picture of Channing lying in bed with just a silk sheet to cover his modesty

"What is wrong with this man?" I silently wonder. How does he think my phone has died if I just sent a text to say goodbye? Obviously, he doesn't understand how to read between the lines! Or technology either, it seems.

For what seemed like a century long week, he messaged. Sending nauseating vomit inducing love songs from YouTube. Odes of everlasting love for me. This is when I realised, I had opened a true Pandora's box. I was out of my depth dealing with someone who may be more than slightly unhinged. My need for entertainment was going to come back and bite me on the bum, with all its teeth gripping and not letting go!

Another photo, and another one, and another one! Hundreds, in fact! Will he ever stop? Usually, I would not mind looking at pictures of Channing, but I was sick of the sight of him now. I could never watch Step Up or 21 Jump Street again. The misery that flashed through my mind at that very moment was unpalpable.

"I remember you said you like baby blue eyes! My eyes are blue. I have to wear contacts when I'm working!" My eyes rolled so far back; I am convinced I looked as though I had a starring role in a low budget zombie movie. Then the picture. Just a cropped picture of his eyes, hiding his identity.

"Gotcha! I know who you are!" I would recognise those eyes anywhere! I had seen them several times. You have tried to get my attention for months on social media. Immediately, you could see that this man was not a body double for anyone, the tiny eyes, surrounded by the chubby features of his face that made them barely visible. Following the eyes pic was the dick pic I wish I had never seen. That nauseous wave overcomes me again. Not sure if I can hold it down this time! The offence to my eyes was absolute! Before me was an uncooked pig in a blanket.

Now that it had gone a step or two too far, I needed to rein this in. Put a stop to it once and for all, so I took the sensible decision and asked him to meet me. Did I mention that rhubarb gin with a dash of lemonade is lush?

"I need you in my life. Please, can I meet you I'm free on Sunday?" I boldly text while gleefully cackling away to myself

Met with silence for 3 days, my attention had turned to a much more attractive prospect, in the shape of Mr Mercedes. Something that had genuine possibilities. Then it came through on Sunday lunchtime. The next part of his cover story.

"I'm so sorry Darling, I didn't see your message," his chubby fingers typed.

"I got a last-minute booking for a cover shoot in Germany

"Are you a catfish?"

"What's a catfish?" he voices notes with a nervous laughter.

Did I respond? No, would be the answer!

Several hours later, he calls. "Sorry, I went to the pub to catch up with some friends. I told them what you asked me, and they did not know what a catfish was. Explain what you are asking," with a genuine confusion in his voice.

After a brief explanation of what a catfish is, he cannot keep denying his deceit.

"I can't believe you think I would do that to you. Your ex-partners have done proper a job on you!" with shock and indignation. "You need to trust men. Not all of us are bad!"

As he is talking, I am slowly scrolling through Google images to find the unedited versions of

Channing Tatum pictures. Forty pictures sent straight back to him while he is still trying to convince me of his honourability.

"I've sent you some pics, babe. I hope you enjoy them as much as I did!" The pause and the silence that confirmed his truth. His lies exposed! The reality of the situation hitting home. The true nature revealed.

"How dare you! You have led me on all this time! You knew all along," he said with such ferocity, I found myself speechless.

"Are you fucking kidding me? You have been lying all the way along and I'm the bad guy?" I exploded. Mr catfish had only seen my gentle side, but my full Caribbean and Irish temper had risen to unrivalled heights. It was all unleashed until he fell into a quiet submission.

"I tried to get your attention as myself, but you never responded, and I just wanted to get to know you," with self-pity dripping from his tongue. The excuse on the other end of the phone made me more disgusted.

"I thought you would be the shallow type, and not want to speak to me because I am fat,"

"No, it's not because I am shallow, it is because YOU have been cyberstalking me for months and you are

a complete weirdo. It is not because you are fat," quietly admitting to myself that it was because he is obese. I do not mind a bit of a dad bod, but I do like my gentlemen on the slimmer side.
BLOCKED!

Now you would think that would be the end of the story, but this one is not giving up. Just to add another twist to the weirdness and tenacity of this one, I received voice messages from Santa. Unbelievable, I know!
"Mr Catfish has been a naughty boy, but he wants you to forgive him and put him back on the good list. After 10 mins of utter nonsense and good old father Christmas ruined for me forever, I unblocked and dialled his number. The complete repulsion I felt while the deafening sound of the phone ringing in my ears was taking me over. He picks up and I hear his voice. What once sounded so sexy was now replaced with a voice that sent chills down my spine. "Hope you liked the message? I wanted to leave you alone for a while, so you could calm down and come to your senses. I will tell you anything you want to know," so calmly, acting as though we were discussing leaving the toilet seat up or down.
"My name is 'Mr Catfish,' and I live in Sheffield and sell e-cigs. I have been single for 10 years,"

"Well, that's not a surprise. Try to stop lying to women and STOP BEING A FUCKING WEIRDO! You might find yourself more successful!" with the blood rising to my face in disbelief and anger. "Try to ring me again or send me messages from Santa, the Easter rabbit or the fucking tooth fairy. I will call the police for harassment."

I think you can guess what happened next. BLOCKED!!

Mr Catfish says....

How many times do I have to swipe her, only to be ignored? With her profile linked to her Instagram, I can see she is real. I want her and will do anything to get her. But would a woman like her even look in my direction? Only one serious relationship in my life, producing my beautiful baby girl. Growing fast, always concerned that I am not happy with my world. She's right. My life revolves around my businesses and going to the pub for a drink with the lads. Afterwards, I go home to my magnolia walls and silence. Filled with noise and chaos every other weekend when my daughter comes to visit. Her mother is a bitch, and that is me putting it politely. She used me to get my house, my money. Once she was pregnant and our angel arrived, her true nature showed. I would have done anything for her. They took all of it from me. Never will I forgive her. Her words cut right through me. If it wasn't the need to care for the princess.

"Fat fuck, you disgust me. I feel sick when you touch me. I just wanted your money," she said. The words tumbling from her tongue with sheer spite.

All I need is a good woman to love me and show my daughter goodness. If she looks like Susanna Reid from GMTV, that would be a bonus. I like slim but curvy brunettes with dark eyes. And I think I've found her. I just need to get her attention and make her fall for my personality first. My ex was right, in one sense. I need to lose a few pounds. I may be no Channing Tatum, but I'm a good guy. Someday, someone will see past the exterior and see the wonderful human beneath, unless they are truly shallow. There seem to be a lot of those types online, but I am sure I can cut through the crap to find the gold. Maybe today is the day she will get back to one of my many messages. I try one more try on Instagram, still no response. I bet she hasn't seen it. She must get loads of guys in her DMs, but I know she is looking. She is still on Tinder.

It's early, decide to stay in bed and have another lazy day. watching Susanna in the morning is always a way to relax me. I can't really hear what she is saying, but I'm horny. It's then my moment of inspiration happens. I'll use someone else's pictures, get her to fall for me, then reveal the true me. It will a fall into place as by then she will become so within deep with her heart, and her emotions and feelings for me, she will not want to turn me away. It's a solid plan. This will not go bad. She will be mine, eyes on the goal.

Some might say our relationship is to be a house of cards based on a lie, but we will prove them all wrong. Hours later scouring the internet for pictures, one man stands out to me. Dare I do it? It's done, no going back. Now I just need to find her within of the sea of faces flashing before me. So much time has lapsed but I see her. I swipe. No one else, just her. Days go by and nothing. It's not working. Why is it not working? Something is wrong. Maybe she's had an accident or, even worse, she has met someone else. That can't be. She is mine. I mean us to be together. MY apartment is feeling smaller by the day, the carpet becoming more threadbare by the minute. I can't stop pacing. I need a cigarette.

Two weeks and at last my phone alerts me to the match of my dreams. I'm going to play it cool. Wait for her to message me first. The seconds turn into minutes, minutes into hours, hours into days. Time passed slowly. I can't eat, sleep or even think straight. I'm going to have to take the first step. My eyes catch my watch and I realise it has, in reality, been only 2 minutes. I'll message anyway. I know she will wait for me to make the first move. She is a lady, and I must be the gentleman to take our relationship to the next level.

"Hey gorgeous, how is your day going? Can't believe you are single?"

"How has your day been, handsome?"

From that first exchange, we connected. We talked until the small hours of the night. All the while I was scouring the net for more pics so I could share more of me with her. Our conversation was open and honest. She was sharing her woes with me, trusted me. Yes, I told her a few white lies, but she would forgive me as I could feel her love towards me. Of this, I am sure.

Every night, I rushed home from work just to talk to her. My thoughts filled with her smile, daydreaming of the life we were going to have together. The staff can sense the changes in me. It's her influence. She is changing me into the man I want to be. Full of confidence and pride in myself. Last night she told me she loves blue eyes, how they pierce her soul when she looks into them and loses herself. My phone editor is in overdrive while I crop a picture of my true self to show her mine. She will never notice it's not the same guy as my profile.

"Your eyes seem so familiar to me, almost like I've seen them before," she says

"Thats just because we are soul mates, already connected before we met,"

"That must be it, talking of meeting. When do you think that will happen?"

The hard chair in my back office is the pit of despair that I feel. I need to work out how I'm going to tell her the truth. I need to at some point if we are going to meet our destiny of being together.

"Soon, my love, soon. I've just got a few things to sort out with work. Let's speak as soon as I get home. I'm out with the lads tonight. I've already told them so much about you and they can't believe a woman like you would be interested in someone like me."

"They are just jealous, because you are super handsome, gorgeous body and amazing personality. They should really say, 'Does she realise what a catch you are, and I hope she appreciates how lucky she is,' I've got to get back to work. I'll speak to later,"

This woman is melting me. She is everything I hoped she would be and more. I will miss her once she is in work mode. I don't hear from her for hours, but I least I can stare at her photos and imagine our first kiss together. It's going to be so special. I send her a link to Whitney Houston's; I will always love you.

It's strange, she hasn't contacted me for hours. The boys are not believing that I have captured this woman's heart; I need her to text. Prove them wrong, and as if on cue, I see her name appear on my phone.

"Are you a catfish?"

"What's one of them?"

Sensing the puzzlement, the loudest one of the group asks what the problem is as he hands me a cold pint. A drink I have been wanting all day.

"She has just called me a catfish! I don't understand. What is one of them?" I said to him. This is not good, judging by his reaction. Just about avoiding the spray of lager and cruel laughter. Not so gently, he explains, as I feel my anger rise towards him. The thought of shoving my fist into his rather large mouth right now is so appealing. Has she worked it out? Can I get round it? Maybe I have gone a bit too far with the Channing Tatum body double story. Think I might leave her for a while so she can't ask too many questions. The night spent boasting of my A grade woman, the lads still in disbelief that such a woman would even glance my way, never mind want to be with me. As the rosy glow of the alcohol and lively atmosphere of the night settle in, my stories become bigger, even my friends taken in by them. Forgetting that, I still must answer her questions to face up to the lies and tales I have created. A message disturbed the most peaceful sleep. Oh shit, she wants to meet me. This will have to be dealt with tomorrow. I need time to think.

Panic setting in, not knowing how to respond, I left her cold for 2 days. She kept checking in to make sure everything was OK. Worried about me; the concern showing through in her texts. The guilt in my heart, warning me I was about to lose her, but my arrogant voice in my chose not to believe this. I was confident because she had fallen in love with me, and she would forgive the initial deception.

Two days felt like 20 years. Not talking to her must be the hardest thing I have ever done in my life. The pain was incompressible. Missing her, it was time to bite the bullet and get in touch. Still not ready to reveal all, considering what to say.

"Sorry babe, I had a last-minute booking for a magazine cover in Germany. Flew out with only an hour's notice,"

"No worries lovely, it's such a shame as I was free on Sunday. I could have driven over. It's such a pleasant drive over the Pennines at this time of year,"

"Gutted, I really want to see," I said, but my next move would be the one to seal the deal. It would forever intrigue her, enable our connection physically. Not only will she want me emotionally, but she will want to place her soft fingers upon me, stroking and bringing me to a heady climax. She will want to please me and keep me happy. The pleasure my hand is bringing, imagining it is her, and finally she takes me into her mouth. Her tongue tasting me with its licks and flicks around my shaft. It takes a while before she responds, probably returning the favour, as I lick my lips lasciviously. Posing in front of the mirror to get a good angle on her naked body. I hope she has tan lines, finding them sexy. She has the confidence to do this for me.

Pictures are coming through. I don't want to see at them just yet. I need to prepare myself for them. The aroma of coffee brewing in my kitchen, the one piece of luxury in my life. I pour and savour the smell from the steam in my nostrils. Settle down in my softest armchair, ready to be pleased by the sight of her.

Not exactly what I was expecting. She has known all along. She has led me on, played with me. What a bitch! The trill beep of my phone driving through my head. Make it stop. I can't take it anymore. Every photo I have ever sent her is flying back to me. The unedited versions. My mistake was thinking I had done enough to disguise the fact it was Channing. The phone ringing for an eternity. I can't answer. The pain in my chest, the breathlessness of my lungs, I'm having a panic attack. She won't stop, the ringing constant. I want the world to go away. How could she be so cruel? To forgive me, I need her to understand.

"I'm so sorry. I just wanted to get your attention. You have ignored me so many times. I just thought that if I could get to know you, you would like me and see past the exterior, but it turns out you are just as shallow as all the rest. Leading me on to see what you could get out of me. Pretending to like me, while all the time leading me on,"

"Charming, you lie to me, pretend to be someone else and I'm the bad guy,"

Stunned at the anger coming at me, furious, I bet she looks cute angry. I can turn this around. She just needs time to think this through.

"I thought we could get through this, that you would accept me for who I truly am. The pictures mean nothing. You like my personality, so what does it matter what I look like? I never thought you would turn on me. You are just like all the rest of the women that I meet. Shallow, materialistic, and mean!"

"Are you fucking kidding me? I'm shallow? And whatever else you said? No, the reason I don't want to be with you is because you are a liar and there is no trust."

"I will never meet the right woman. "

"Stop feeling sorry for yourself. Try to stop lying and stop being a fucking weirdo!"

To say I had pissed her off might be a bit of an understatement. There will be a resolution. I live with hope and positivity. Blind hope, you might say.

As soon as the line disconnected, I looked on in horror at the message thread. How could I have been so stupid to think a woman like her would like me? She's gone, her photo has gone. Why would she block me? Devastated, I search Instagram, Facebook, twitter, searching for her social media accounts. All have disappeared. All this time, she knew my true identity. I need to get in touch with her. Two weeks of loneliness, pacing my bedroom floor, constantly checking my phone went by. My life was so empty without her, the coldness in my heart returning, what I would give to hear her laugh one more time.

A brilliant idea, it's coming to the festive season, and everyone is happy this time of year. My messages are still not going through, but she can't refuse a call from the big man, Santa, himself. He can apologise on my behalf. A few moments later, her picture reappeared.

"Try to ring me again or send me messages from Santa, the Easter rabbit or the fucking tooth fairy. I will call the police for harassment."

Not the reaction I was hoping for. Her picture, once again, disappeared before my eyes

Mr Mercedes

I am on my knees praying, looking up at the skies. Pleading with the online dating gods to send me someone that just resembles some sort of normal. This swiping malarkey was not as easy as I first imagined. The belief of finding my Mr Right online was fast fading into disappointment. As the menopause is taking effect, I am thinking there is no hope for me. The heatwave is at its highest alongside the hot flushes. I can feel the sweat trickling down my forehead as I am swiping, or was that the anticipation that my blind faith brings me? There he is! Olive skinned, 5 o'clock shadow, a nice firm jawline, with a smile that gave you that a warm wet feeling in your pants. Mr Mercedes, with his devilish grin, looking like he would devour me through the screen of my phone. Sat on the front seat of his Merc wearing a white shirt and black tie showing the outline of his muscular arms and chest. Tentatively, I swipe right. Yes! It's a match! Play cool, do not be too eager! The menopausal beast has awoken!

For a while it was as if I was talking to myself same sense of humour and conversation style.

Double entendre flowing everywhere in a furiously fast text conversation. There was never any thought of our relationship with this man. I just know he was sexy, and I had to have him. Still playing by the dating game rules, waiting for him to make the first move. Playing the feminine role, letting him lead with his masculine energy. After a week of nonsensical chatter and laughter, he asked if he could pop round in on his way home from work, which was conveniently only 5 minutes away from the house.

Frantically, I run around the house, trying to make myself more presentable, instead of the sweaty mess. It's 25 degrees outside and my only choice after looking through my pitiful excuse of a wardrobe is my faithful denim shorts and a cute lemon vest. To bra or not to bra, that is the question? It is too hot to be strapped into an underwired contraption. They seem to do an excellent job on their own, even if they are a tad excited, pressing against the soft cotton of my vest.

There is just no time for make-up. A quick dash to the dressing table to rummage through my assortment of serums, vials, and creams. Could I be a little fresher, slapping a load of products all over my face? Toner, serums, moisturiser, and sunscreen revealing a dewier youthful look. Note to self. Stop matching with men 10 years younger than yourself. It will be hard, as men my age cannot seem to manage my energy or my humour. Why do men get so uptight as they get older? Where is the fun in that?

That heady mix of anxiety and excitement as I nervously keep glancing through my bedroom window during my rushed preparations. There is nothing more I can do now, as he has not exactly given me a lot of notice. The road is empty and quiet, and then I see it gleaming in the sun, the sleekness of a C class Mercedes in bright white driving towards my house. The gentle purr of the engine, in rhythm with my pounding heartbeat. He is here! I pause, waiting for him to announce his arrival.

Shoes! Where the fuck are my shoes? No choice. I saunter out of the house barefooted. Wild curls bouncing in the slight breeze, a welcome cool on my skin. A blush come over my face as I see him. Suddenly, my shyness has kicked in. Awkwardly, I stroll over to the car, which was less than 3 metres away but felt like miles. Sat against the car bonnet nonchalantly, with a big grin appearing on his face as soon as he saw me.

At once, I felt at ease with him, even though I could feel the danger and urgency coming from him. He pulled me towards me with a firmness that displayed his confidence. Finally, someone wanted to kiss me, and I was not about to resist. I gave into the touch of his lips on mine. The sexual tension between us was instant. Not usually caring for PDAs, I felt abandonment of my usual fears and cares. He was just what I needed at this point in my life. I could feel his desire for me through that kiss. I welcomed the warm flush that crept up over my body, as I stepped back from him while looking into his face. Our expressions mirroring each other.

Sat in the front seat of his car, the conversation was as easy as text. Comfortable in his space, I leant over and gave him a kiss full of promise and intention. The need to have him was urgent, but there was no way I was having sex with this insanely handsome man that smelled so good in his car parked in front of my house. I could feel his hands wander over my body and it was responding to him. No matter how hard I tried, I couldn't hide it. I pulled away and bid him goodbye. This was to be continued another day. Little did I know it would be less than 24 hours before that promise came to fruition.

As soon as he arrived home, he messaged. There were no sex texts or rude emojis. He didn't need them! He knew exactly what he was doing and how to do it. If there was ever a man who understands his sexuality, then I had just met him. He didn't feel predatory or sleazy. Mr Mercedes could take flirting to a whole new level. How to make a woman want him, without needing to communicate that he wasn't looking for the love of his life. He just wanted your body and to enjoy the entire process.

I am really going to change that notification sound. It's 6 am, Sunday morning, for Christ's sake. I rouse from my slumber to check my phone through blurred vision. What the fuck is he doing? Standing proudly in a wetsuit at a lake, showing every part of his body as it clung, leaving nothing to the imagination. What the hell? Laughing, and wondering what he was like without the suit. "What are you up to? Busy day?"

"I was thinking about you and was going to pop round? Maybe we could go for a walk?"

It's just too early to make these sorts of rational decisions, so I made an irrational one. "See you at 1pm" followed by the winking emoji. Every fibre of my being told me I was just about to be taken out of my vanilla comfort zone. After today, I could no longer perceive at myself in the same way. Was my public exterior of being an average everyday suburban middle-aged homemaker about to disappear? I felt the sense of adventure swelling within me, the need to follow the danger. It's time to pull myself out of my drowning lake of normality. At least this time I have a bit more time to prepare, but I'm easily distracted.

This heat is incredible, sat in just my knickers and vest, doing my daily check in on socials. Why does it appear to be that everyone is getting into new relationships, making a commitment to someone? All I wanted to achieve was to find that person who will take away the long, lonely nights, dinners at posh restaurants, curling up in front of the TV and yet here I sit, still single. I need to switch off. Find a distraction from my hot flushes and impending doom of spinsterdom! Absorbed in a mind-numbing textbook for one of the many courses I thought would be all about my journey and quest for self-improvement. Reggae playlist on in the background. Damian Marley "Beautiful" brings me to my senses. "Alexa, what time is it?" "12.37pm!" I've done it again and left myself with no time to get ready. Menopausal brain fog at full effect.

Laid back casual is the only way to go! Little denim mini skirt, favourite pair of Adidas superstars, white shirt that's too big and falls gently off the shoulder, revealing but just enough. A little skin can go a long way! Final once over in the lean-to mirror, I like the way I'm looking. All those hours in the gym and the garden are paying off. With heart pumping and nervous knots in my stomach, I stroll out of the house as though I don't have a care in the world. His smile blindsides me. Should have worn sunglasses as his teeth are way too bright, against the reflection of the sun. Eyes straining in the glare, I smile back, followed by a nervous giggle. Tentatively, I allow him to take my hand, fingers entwined as he leads me to his car. "I thought we were going for a walk?"

He holds open the back car door for me and he slides into the driver's seat. We drive for 5 mins and pull into the local cemetery. Not exactly what I had in mind for a romantic rendezvous? What is going through his mind? I'm slightly confused. I can see his face in the rear-view mirror. His smile has turned into a salacious, devilish grin. Uh oh! I am in trouble. I can feel the thrill of excitement run through me. It's trouble that I am happy to be involved in.

He pulls over just behind the graveyard church and joins me in the back seat. The windows are almost black, shutting out the rest of the world. My sensory awareness is dissipating, along with my inhibitions.

As his hand snakes its way up my shirt, he pulls me to sit astride him. So glad I forgot to put my knickers on. He slides into me with ease. Bit unexpected, but I'm going with it. My head banging on the roof of the car, my hips grinding against his. I can feel his fullness inside me. The sounds of passers-by shoes crunching on the gravel paths only added to the excitement and intensity. The danger of being heard or caught. My mind flashing to the door locks, hoping he had remembered to active them. Half-naked bodies glistening in the heat of the car and condensation forming on the windows. We climax together as I collapse onto his hard body, head resting on his shoulders. We take a minute to regain our breath and realise the enormity of what just happened. Did we really just have sex in the graveyard?

As I climb off him to pull myself together and straighten up my clothes, I hear his voice. It sounded a million miles away, bringing me back to reality with a harsh slap.

"That was lush! Fancy doing it again sometime?" he remarked.

Lush? He's just ruined the moment. Who calls passionate sex in the back of a Merc in the middle of a graveyard "lush"? I'm not sure if I could disguise my contempt for such a remark. We made sure we were presentable and went for the promised walk. The graveyard was peaceful and pretty, with the sun shining through the leaves of the trees. I forgive him for the use of the word and laugh along with the male version of myself.

We met up with each other the next night. At his home, for normal bedroom sex, nothing exciting to report. I left, went to a friend's house for a glass of cheap wine, and went home. I didn't contact him again for 6 months. Still single and a girl has needs. And I knew I could make his lunchtimes much more interesting!

Mr Mercedes says....

I've been told many times that I'm super sexy and there are too many women in this world to sleep with. But I can give it a good go. I spend many a night on all the dating apps and socials, trawling the murky waters of dating in my forties. Take last night, for example, I friend requested approximately fifty women, followed the same amount on the gram. Some respond, some don't. Now I know they like me; many think I'm fit, and I am! As soon as they ask my height, I'm off. Been there before. They all want a 6 foot 4 Adonis. Ladies, there are not enough of them in the world to keep you all happy. Good things come in small packages. That doesn't mean everything about me is small.

Since splitting from the missus, my priority is my kids. I love the company in the female form and if it leads to a bit of bedroom action, then all the better. Many of the women I meet are really uptight. Sense of humour failure and the biggest negative. They want to drag me down the aisle and force me into some sort of suburban nightmare and boring sex. That's fine for them, not for me. I'm enjoying the playground that Tinder allows. There are few that left a lasting impression. Bringing a smile to my face, with the sheer memories. Women who brought a bit of spice and adventure to our unions. The experience in the graveyard is up there with the best of them.

I will not bore you with all the usual claptrap about how I saw her whilst swiping and how she stood out from the crowd. I was just randomly swiping, to see what hit. When I match, I'm like a rat down a sewer pipe. You must get in quick. The ladies love it. They think you are really excited to have a chance with them. Little do they know; they are one of several that night. If you respond, I'll chat with you. Of course, I don't tell them my intentions. I allow them to believe in me. No one wants a fuck boy. I've got two phones, one for my everyday life of work and kids, and one for dating. Anybody who is as prolific as me with these apps should treat it this way. You are a fool if you don't keep these two lives separate. Ingenious of me if you really think about it. I can go on a date and give my woman off the hour my full undivided attention, and if she is not worth meeting again, I can see if there are any messages from more prospects when I get home. I'm not looking for the love of my life, but I obviously don't share this information with the beautiful ladies of the dating apps.

Let's talk about Miss Graveyard. I knew almost instantly that this one would be a little wild within moments of our conversation starting. You get a feel for these things. I've had enough practice. Need to take my time, not jump straight to the point, rein her in. Just hoping she is not vanilla, had too many of those, all wanting hearts and flowers when all I want is some no holds barred excitement. It took about a week if memory serves me right. Sorry, they all blend into one. Anyway, I got her to agree to meet me after work outside her house. The task wasn't hard. I had a goal in mind and as I also meet my sales targets at work; I pursue my dating life in the same way. Armed with a pocket full of condoms, sure that I was going to score this afternoon, I drove manically towards her house. Dictated a text to her phone to tell her I had arrived, losing my nerve. Need to brazen this out. As the weather was on my side, I leant against the bonnet of my car and waited. She was taking her time, obviously making herself beautiful for me. Not really into the full make-up overdone appearance, but they all turn up looking like they had spent the afternoon in the Selfridges beauty department having a makeover. I look up and there she is, striding towards me. Her natural beauty was obvious, but what struck me the most was how carefree she seemed. Her curls dancing in the breeze, with the same bounce as her braless breasts straining against the soft fabric of her vest. If they were that desperate to escape, I was positive I could give them a helping hand and speed up the process. Think of me as the boob libertarian. This one differed from the rest; she wasn't even wearing shoes. I need to be careful as I think I could grow to like this one. Sex oozing from her, she leans in, and her lips brush my cheek. Instantly immersed in her scent, faint notes of orange and wood. My favourite Paco Rabanne perfume, Olympea, filling my space. The sounds of the main road dissipating as my eyes feast upon her. My dick appreciating the sight of her, my hardness becoming visible in my trousers.

As she pulls away, I take charge and kiss her. Met with a brief resistance, she caves and responds to my lips. As kisses go, this was a good one. We need somewhere more private. And I don't think she is ready for me to enter her home. Gently guiding her to the passenger seat of the car, I know she is going to be impressed with the newness of the Merc. The only miles on the clock were the ones to her house.

There is nothing better than the smell of a new car. The leather interior is enough to set the scene for sex.

I love her laugh, its genuine as are her smiles, its infectious, Sat in the relative privacy of the car, pedestrians strolling past with no knowledge of what was about to happen. I go in for the kill, passionate kisses as my hands wander over her curves. What an arse! This one is in good shape for her age. I rarely go for the older woman, too many flabby bits, but she takes care of herself. She has a confidence that shows she knows this. The power of her flirt is getting me excited, and I want her now. Why is she stopping me? I'm ready to go. Another attempt to get my hand between her legs as my kisses grow stronger. She stops me and redirects to her waist, It's so bloody frustrating! I need to pull myself together, hold back, make her want me. "I need to go," I say with a sharp sting in my tongue.

Was that surprise or disappointment that showed on her face for a fleeting moment? She needs to understand that if I don't go now, there is no holding me back. My persistence will prevail. I will have her just once to satisfy my curiosity. I can conquer this fine example of a female curiosity before me. Certain she will crack and give in to her needs, I pull away from reluctantly taking my hand off her backside.

Climbing back into my car, knowing I'm going to have to get home fast. My dick urgently needs some self-love. Driving away, I quickly dictate a text to her, "Same time tomorrow? We could go for a walk?" "Would love to!" she said as I imagine her voice was speaking and not the generic voice of Siri. Knowing that she will have a broad smile on her face. It's almost a shame to not let her get to know me, because this will be a onetime thing only. Those are my rules. I cannot get involved with anyone. I don't want it and I don't need it! All the drama that comes with relationships. It's just more than I can bear at this time of my life. I'm happy being single, having my space, but my body has cravings and needs to be met.

Morning swims outdoors, just as the sun is rising must be my favourite activity after random sex. My performance is lacking today as my senses heightened with the slow currents of the lake and the earth cold beneath my feet, mud running through my toes. The wetsuit keeping me from feeling the artic temperature of the water. The sun creeping up behind the hills, creating a mirage of rainbows against the murky water. I grab a passing swimmer to take a picture and send it. I know it's 6 am, but she will be fine with it. She will receive a present this afternoon, so I need to show her the goods. What's on offer!

"WTF are you doing? You are mental," she says, followed by a laughing emoji.

Good start. I did not piss her off at all. Sense of humour is so sexy in a woman.

"I will see you at one," I said. "Looking forward to seeing you,"

It was all true. I was looking forward to getting her in the back of my car and having my wicked way with her. I knew that there was no way she was going to let me in her home, and I wasn't ready to bring her to mine.

It's so hot but feeling good from the morning lake swim. It clears my head and I try to get a swim in every morning. Lightweight t-shirt and cargo shorts. No belt, I need easy access for what I have planned. Just as I'm pulling up outside her house, Damian Marley, "Beautiful," is playing on the radio. Not a big fan of reggae, flip the channel and retro dance music blasts. Now this is more my vibe, the beat in time with my heart, raising my pulse as it gets faster after the bridge. I escape into my imagination of the day ahead and there she is in my rear-view mirror. Once again, no make-up. What is it with this chick? She just doesn't seem to care what people think about her. She looks amazing, with no effort put in at all. At least this time she is wearing shoes. She slides into the back seat as I guided her, watching her tanned legs circle into the car. I am getting a rock-solid boner. Where can I take her? That's not too far? I need to be serviced. She leans over and gives me a kiss. The type of kiss that tells me I am getting lucky today. With a quizzical look at me as I drive, but also slightly intrigued "I thought we were going for a walk" she said.

All I can do is smirk at her through the mirror. Driving for five minutes until we arrive at our destination, loving the shock on her face that she cannot hide. It's peaceful, pretty, and quiet. I pull the car around the back of the church and join her in the rear seat. The way she looks at me is endearing and full of want. While squeezing her tits, I pull her astride me. Dick already escaped from my shorts. I guide her onto my fine member of manhood. Instant relaxation. Her tits bouncing in my face, head banging on the roof of the car. The blacked-out windows were wet with condensation from the heat of our bodies. I grip her curves as while she tries to place her palm on the window to gain her balance. It's only just occurred to me how small the back of my car is? Together we come, and I feel her full weight collapse on me. Both spent and exhausted. "That was lush" I said.

Her attitude seemed to change towards me, almost like she was now done with me. I'm not taking that very well. No-one has ever used me for sex. It makes me want her again. I can win her round by taking her on that walk I promised her. There was an unspoken comfort between us as we strolled through the shade of the trees holding hands.

As I drove home, I knew I was going to see her again. Didn't realise it would be the next night. Fear was building within me. If I wasn't careful, this was going to end up as a relationship. The next night she visited me, we had sex. Nothing nearly as exciting as the day before, but it still felt right. As she left my house that night, she said goodbye, and I knew she meant it. That was it until I got a text from the stranger.

"What are you doing this lunchtime? Fancy popping round and I'll make you something to eat?" she said. Put it this way, lunchtimes just got a lot more interesting!

Mr Prisoner

I found not all my pseudo romances online. I am more than capable of entering into a fucked-up relationship all by myself, even when I've met them in the flesh. This is a special talent of mine. It's taken some time to fine tune my skills in this department, but lI reckon I am world class. If a male wants to approach me, please have your red flags waving away. The more the better, as I'm likely to be attracted to you. So, let's grab a coffee and get yourself ready for this one.

Sitting on the side of the pool, immersed in the echoes and the incessant chatter of my best friend, I see him out of the corner of my eye. Vaguely familiar, but I can't place. Where do I know him from? Still handsome from memory, I watch him climb the ladder to replace a lightbulb. Now I come to think of it, there were four of them. All doing the job with ineptitude. It couldn't possibly be him. There is no way on this earth that this man would work at the local pool, doing crappy maintenance. I could imagine him running the company, maybe with a small amount of fear from his employees, but being the dogsbody? Nah! No Way! Never! Old age creeping up on me, blurred vision. I must be in my imagination. Note to self, make an appointment at the opticians, it's time for an eye test and just accept that your vision disappeared at the same time as your periods. It's a good job you hit the gym regularly, otherwise you would have a bum on top of a layer of droopy skin, just like some of the fine examples you see surrounding yourself in their boring swimsuits with tummy control panels. Need to get out of my head. Focus on the matter at hand. Is it him? The deliciously dangerous man you are besotted with all those years ago. The man you who would walk into a room, and you would become a complete dickhead, a stuttering mess.

"I need to go. There is something I forgot to do," I said to the BF. Careful not to slip, running to the dressing rooms, like my arse was on fire. Breathless, running after me, enquiring "Are you Ok? What's happened? "

"Nothing, I just need to get out of here. Feel like I can't breathe,"

The journey home did nothing to allay my thoughts. Even the dulcet tones of Dennis Brown could calm me down. Me and Dennis, we've been through a lot together. He is always there when I need him, but not on this occasion. It was making it worse. Dennis was his favourite reggae artist. I remembered vaguely him telling me once, while I was trying to build up the Dutch courage to talk to him, by downing nearly an entire bottle of his friends, Remy Martin. The embarrassment I felt thirty years ago was hitting me as waves of nausea. The same feeling as the moment he found me, head over the toilet bowl, doing a great impersonation of the exorcist. He scooped me up and drove me home to my city centre apartment. The pity I felt for myself was unpalatable. I could feel myself shrinking farther and farther into myself. How had I got myself into such a mess, especially in front of him? He will never look at me and seems to be attracted to me.

He was the strong, silent type, but there was a good reason for that. His reputation was fearsome, and he was one of the city's biggest mobsters. But for me, I have never felt safer in a man's company. He was gentle in the way he spoke to me, caring as he escorted me to my front door and made sure I got home safely. Many a man would have taken advantage of a young drunk woman, especially if they knew she fancied them. It was a free leg over, with no hard work. But not him. He was a complete gentleman. He didn't look at me with disgust, repulsion, or leer. It was genuine concern I could see in his eyes. Or was I just completely pissed? It was a combination of both.

Forever seeing him around town. Popping into the bar, I worked with regular frequency. I'm not sure if it was my bikini we had to wear as a uniform that made him a regular, or it had become his new office, so to speak. Never allowing himself to be served by anyone else but me. My confidence growing as I could see him become nervous in my presence, hearing his friends full of laughter teasing him. Through his closest allies, we somehow had many a conversation, finding out about each other, eventually leading to the confirmation of a date. People around town warning me to stay away from him, to leave well alone. I couldn't be told. They didn't know him, they just listened to rumours circulating.

Waking up to the loudness of the landline, fall out of bed and make my way to the living room, feeling slightly queasy. It's bloody 5am in the morning, I've only had three hours sleep after a late shift on the bar. Confused at the New York accent on the phone and with the conversation I was trying desperately to keep up with.

"We will send a car for you, you will fly first class on the red eye,"
Wait! What? Did I fall asleep on the phone? I've agreed to something. I don't have a clue to where I am going, but I'm nodding my head as I climb back into bed. It felt like only 5 minutes had passed before I'm awoken again by the phone. This time, it's the chauffeur to confirm what time he is picking me up. It's all coming back to me now. I auditioned for a job, supporting a pop star, but they want me to choreograph her next video instead. Shit, I'm going to the States in a couple of hours. Dream job, dream career. Finally, it's happening. I don't have time to let anyone know. They will just have to deal with it. In those days we didn't have social media, it was pagers to contact. I had a mobile phone, but no one else did. It would work out, unless I just be dramatic and let them think I've just upped and left. No one would even miss me, while I am off living my best life. So young, and even then, jaded and worn down with the single life.

I stayed for years, going from one job to another, building my career, meeting fascinating people, working constantly, but having no time for a relationship. Too tired to even enjoy the social scene and many parties people in the industry invited me to. I got offered the chance to star in a porn film, though, while in sunny Los Angeles. Apparently, I have a glorious face for blow jobs! Why didn't I come to that conclusion before whenever I looked in the mirror? Is that where I have been going wrong all these years? All I wanted was a candle from a cute little boutique on La Cienaga Blvd, to send home to the mother, but turns out the salesclerk was an aspiring porn director. I left without a candle or a starring role after I threatened to kick him in the nuts, chop it off and feed it to the coyotes roaming the glorious Hollywood hills.

Fast forward, twenty years later, our paths cross again. All the feelings and overwhelming nervousness are still there. The inability to speak in his presence. Not impressed with me about standing him up. As much as I try to explain the situation, it's hard to get it across in the nightclub with the intrusion of the darkness infused with laser lighting and the boom of the speakers. A pen appears from nowhere, making marks on my arm. A date agreed, a fresh start.as I stare at the scribbles left on my skin from the night before, with hungover eyes the next morning, trying to recollect the memories of the night before. Content, cuddling the pillow, I attempt to drift back to sleep with sweet dreams, but not being able to decide if I need to hug the toilet or have a full English. URGH, I need to stop drinking; it gets worse as I get older. Recovery time takes forever.

Date night, I need to present as a sophisticated lady, full of class, unobtainable even if the truth is he can have me in any which ways he wishes. Little black dress lightly accessorised with killer heels, perfect for a dinner date at the hottest restaurant in the city centre. A five-minute walk from my apartment, which should be enough time to pull myself together, get a drink to calm the trembling hands. One drink turned into another as I waited for his arrival, which never came. That night spent once again cuddling the pillow but with my tears and mascara staining the fresh white cotton. The feelings of embarrassment and humiliation, too apparent the next morning. Heartbroken, refusing to answer the door or phone. A hot mess in pyjamas and dressing gown, a DVD of Marley and me on the TV screen, doing nothing but add to the pile of strewn tissues building a wall around my cold feet.

Our paths were to cross again. It's back to the gym. Still stunned, he could have this effect on my being. Images of him with his curly hair, sparkling eyes, and the best smile ever to engrave my mind, stubborn in my memory. Last time it was so innocent, my thoughts about him were pure, but now with my life experiences, my thoughts could now send me to hell. Don't know why I am worried, there are only two outcomes. A. it wasn't him, B. if it was, he was only there for one day so would never see him again. Relieved, wearing my ugliest swimsuit, one that was designed for swimming, not posing, I make my way to the steam room. Dissolve the tension I'm feeling in my muscles, exactly what I needed.

"Babes, I knew it was you," he said as though no time at all had passed. Mortified! Scrunching the surrounding towel to become a corset and protector, fully aware of the fact that I was semi naked underneath.

"Hi, I thought it was you. Sorry, I have forgotten your name. What was it again?"

"You know my name. Stop being stupid. I didn't mean to stand you up. I got waylaid,"

My anger to towards him rising, flabbergasted at how nonchalant he was about this. Just a quick text or phone call would have put me out of my misery instead of the public display of being stood up.

"Babes, don't be angry. It was totally out of my control,"

"You stood me up, and I've not heard from you in over 6 years. Then you stand in front of me like nothing happened. What could you have possibly been doing that stopped you from calling me? If you didn't want to see me, you should have just let me know."

Why is he laughing? As petulant as I am being, he could at least show a little empathy.

"I was arrested and have been in prison ever since. I am working here on day release. Meet me for a coffee at 4pm when I finish, and I will explain everything."

Sat waiting in the coffee shop, with a million questions running through my mind. Do I stay and hear him out? Why are you even thinking about entertaining this man? He's a convicted criminal, so why are you not running and staying well away? Why am I even contemplating this? No man has ever made me feel nervous the way he does. It's not the nerves of meeting someone new, it's difficult to explain, but I feel like he is my soulmate. Never have I had these feelings for someone. We have had many sliding door moments. Maybe now I need to open the door and go through, making sure we are both going through the same one.

As I see him walk towards me, purposely trying not to look at me, mentally I scold myself for smiling at him. He is just so beautiful, and when I look at him, no words need to be spoken. The feelings are too real and all-encompassing, taking over any control I have of myself. My gut tells me he knows me, how I think, joke, and react to the world around me. For two hours, we talked until his transport turned up to take him back to his imprisonment. Can I remember what we said between us? No, but I know my decision to continue became confirmed. Never in a million years did I ever dream or expect I would become a prison wife. I wanted him, have done all the years I've known him, buried away, but now I am ready.

For the next year, we met every day for coffee. We never discussed what was going to happen when he was a free man. In our previous life, I knew he was always at the risk of being sent down. Every Tuesday night, around 9.30pm, he would call me. A routine we had fallen into, and I was always there for him, making sure my diary was clear. Letters written with our complete selves exposed. He was allowing me in, showing a side that most never got to see. His pain and fears and vulnerabilities shared with me. Here was a man that half the city felt scared of, untouchable, but here I was, there in the inner sanctum of his thoughts. He could be clumsy sometimes with his approach. If you saw him in the street, you would never imagine him to be the man with his reputation. Almost Urban myth.

No holds barred. The love and bond forming between us was incredible. Each call and letter bringing us closer, but I could hear it in his voice. Something was wrong, and I knew what it was. I had heard the rumours. We are both well known in our city, so it didn't take long for the reports to come back to me. He needed to tell me for himself. Once told though, there was no going back.

"We need to talk. Without making you aware of the situation, I can't continue."

"I don't want to hear it," I said whilst holding back the tears.

"I just want to chat about the normal stuff. The bits that are just about you and me!"

"My ex has been to visit me this week. She wants me to move back in with her. I told her a one-bedroom flat organised, and that I needed to turn my life around. "

"But she hasn't come to see you the whole time you have been away. Never written or brought the kids to see you. Suddenly she wants you back?"

"I will not do it. I will plan with her to see the kids so I can get to know them properly. That's something I need to do!"

"This has to be the most heart-breaking thing I am ever going to say, but I think you need to give that relationship a go. It needs a chance. Your kids deserve them. Everything that has happened was because of you. It's not their fault. You have the paradox of choice, so I will help make it easier for you. Don't call me again!"

Every night for the next two weeks at exactly 9.30pm, my phone would ring and all I could do was stare at it. My heart was now a frozen lake as I walked through each day like a zombie. I would not allow myself to cry, but I wondered if I was ever going to laugh again., and if I did, would I stop peeing myself? Age is a wonderful thing, so I did what any sensible middle-aged woman would do. I bought a cat!

I need to shake this feeling of being in the doldrums off, accepting the invitation to a charity ball. Part of the city's social calendar hosting the rich and the famous. It would be good to attend for my career and to get me out of this bloody house. As I see myself in the mirror, with a glam makeover, I still feel that deep sadness of love lost. Tonight, I will put my best sexy foot forward and smile my way through the evening. Dressed to the nines in a floor length evening gold evening gown, complete with train, plunging neckline and a front split that is a couple of millimetres from me losing all dignity. Bottles of free champagne flowing, the arrogance of alcohol enveloping me — nothing can touch me. Truth be told, I was more than a little drunk than I was steaming. Drunk enough to want to go to the after party. Wise decision? No! Best decision? Absolutely! As I made my way down the stairs of the club, it took a moment to acclimatise myself to my new surroundings. His smile bringing me to a new sense of self-awareness. I fell into his arms for a moment with the force of being run over before realisation dawned on me and hit me by a freight train. He wasn't mine, never would be.

Guiding me over to the bar, we took over the corner and talked. My lack of sobriety hit me once again, giving me a newfound confidence with him. How could I make him stay with him? The decisions we make when we have one too many beverages will come back to haunt us the next morning. I did what any sensible, respectable lady of a certain age would do. I let my hand sneak down towards the zip of his jeans, open it up and slide my fingers to wrap around his balls. They stayed there for the rest of the even and I could see the way he looked at me change. He wanted me. The desire in his eyes was apparent, but tinged with a look of guilt and sadness. My head was spinning from the mixture of champagne and vodka. The need to be near him makes me stay. The night is winding down, and once again, just like he did all those years ago when we first met, he picks me up and takes me home in a black cab. Of course, I invite him inside, but he politely declines. As I watch the black cab pull away, for the final I watch the back of his head move further away from me.

Mr Prisoner says...

There was something different about this one. I shouldn't go near her. Many have said she is too good for me, and I should not be punching above my weight. But I am drawn to her. I see her out and about in the bars in the city centre and can't help staring at her. Do not really care if she catches me, which she often does, then looks the other way. She draws me in. I know little about her and neither does anyone else when I ask around. Sometimes you see her all the time, then nothing for months. I would try to figure out who she was, making up stories in my imagination. Maybe she was the daughter of a crime lord and runs errands for him, or maybe she is a rich older man's plaything and has to entertain him. She is only in it for the money, though. Or she is a petty criminal, always being sent to the local women's prison for her misdemeanours. This is how I entertain myself, by people watching and making up cool stories about them full of adventure and espionage.

Fearless is usually the word that is used to describe, treat life by taking by the devil's balls and squeezing the life out of them, but she terrifies the life out of me. Flash backs to puberty occur when she is in the vicinity, unable to speak or control my body. A jabbering wreck who stutters in her presence, giggling at everything she says. The harder I try to be cool, the more I'm not. She has an ease about her for her young age. Nothing seems to concern her. That's the one thing I would love to be, but in my chosen career path, I am always watching over my shoulder. Dating women, I know I can never make a commitment to. There are plenty of those that are attracted to me with my line of work. There is always plenty of money, free entry to the VIP section of the best clubs, along with dinners and other benefits. The moment I find out about the new bar she is working from; it becomes my local. Every day, I visited, disappointment seeping in on days she wasn't working. But still I went, hoping I would eventually pull myself together and ask her out on a date with me.

The boys think all of this is funny as they have never seen me go to pieces over a woman. One of them decides it would be funny to invite her to an after party without my knowledge. I needed to get her out of her. This wasn't the safest of places for her. A room full of gangsters who didn't care about and might even bring her some harm. She's gone. Bloody hell, she cannot be walking around this area on her own. Anything could happen to her. Making strides to leave the apartment, I glance into the bathroom and there she is in all her glory with head over the toilet bowl, not looking the most attractive I've ever seen her but somehow endearing to me. The need to protect her is immense as I hold back her hair so she can finish vomiting and try to regain her composure.

Too drunk to stand steady, there is only one thing for it. Scooping her up into my arms, she is limp and light as a feather. Her fragility surprises me as I place her in the car and take her home. Any lesser man would have taken advantage of this drunken beauty before me as she invited me into her home. All I wanted was to make sure she was safe and warm in bed. At that precise moment, I made the decision that I was always going to take care of her and not allow her to want for anything. I waited until she had fallen asleep, watched her deep breaths in slumber, which is creepy, I admit, but I am sure she will remember nothing in the morning. For months, I keep going on to that bar until the courage to ask her on a date came to me.

Two hours I waited for her at that restaurant, and she didn't appear. Have a read this all wrong? The sense that we were on the same page was real. I know it was! Why has she stood me up? No one stands a man like me up. They wouldn't dare!

On a night out, chatting to my latest date, I see her. It's got to be twenty years since I waited at the bar for her. The years have been kind to her. She still looks good. I can't stop staring at her. It's dark in this club, with the haze of the smoke machine. Maybe my eyes are just playing tricks on me. I must know why she stood me up that night, or is it I just want to talk to her? As she passes by, our eyes catch. Time stands still for just a moment until I have the nerve to speak without a stutter. Amazed that she still has the power of me to make me into a mumbling mess. I try to hear what she is saying, unable to hear the explanation of why I sat waiting at that bar. I grab a pen from the barman and scribble a time, date, place, and my number on her arm. Confident that she will turn up.

Only a couple of days until the agreed meeting was to happen, but my instinct was talking to me. The feeling of dread, something bad, is going to take place. I can't shake it, and I'm usually a glass half full type of guy.

5am, the sound of the door crashing through startles me and my pregnant girlfriend from our sleep. Time moving slowly. I can't hear the words. With blurred vision, I can make out the shape of the figures before me. Surrounding the bed with guns aimed at my head. Whilst my partner is screaming, shaking with visible fear.

"Keep your hands where we can see them," said the sergeant in charge of the raid. I knew his face. He had arrested several of my gang.

"It's Ok, just arrest me and leave my girl out of this. She has nothing to do with this."

That's not completely true. She knew about my business, enjoyed spending the money and here she was acting as if this was a complete shock to her, portraying the innocent, betrayed partner. Our relationship, volatile and toxic. The lifestyle suited her; harder than any woman I've ever met. The creak of the door on the wardrobe alerted me to my future. A future behind bars. They had found the stash.

"I am arresting you on suspicion of conspiracy to sell class A drugs and for possession of a firearm with ammunition."

Surrender is the only option available to me now. Handcuffs placed around my wrists, tight enough to leave marks, as I'm escorted to the black Moriah van waiting to take me to the nearest police station. There is no way I can get out on time for that date. Will she ever forgive me? I was ready to turn my life around if she wanted to become involved. But why would she? She would soon find out what a low life I am. How do I get word to her without her feeling disgust towards me?

I'm coming to the end of my sentence, early release impending because of good behaviour. No longer in a prison with concrete as far as the eye can see, with bars impairing your vision of the world outside through a small window. Many nights I lie on my cot with plenty of time to think, staring at the stained cold walls. Changes need to be made. It's now or never. My support worker believes I can make those changes with some hard work put in. Several qualifications behind me, they score me a job and some work experience at a gym near my home. Conditions that need to be met are simple. Attend every day, be polite, make sure I do everything that is asked of me and come out as a better person and some money in the bank ready for release with new skills. The world has changed a lot since my incarceration. For one, I will be single for the first time in my life. Social media is a thing now, although I have absolutely no interest in this. Regardless of what you think of me, I am a quiet man, not a fan of too much attention. I keep my words and my thoughts to myself. The job is boring, but it gets me out of the cell for the day and I get to interact with people who know nothing about me. Often getting asked why I was removed from society, which worries me, as most think I am lovely, and I don't want their opinions of me to change. I felt shame, but I can't change it, just make sure I work on improving myself.

Today has been a strange day. It transported me back to the past with no hint that it may be coming. Keeping my composure while up a ladder the size of an oak tree to change a light bulb in the pool area. Maybe it was my imagination and mind playing tricks on me, or maybe a dream. She still looks good after all these years. As hard as I try not to, I can feel myself staring at her as she walks towards the pool, laughing and joking with a man who obviously spends too much time in the gym. The jealousy gives me a tight feeling in my chest and the swell of anger rising. I have no right to feel this way. Not sure if she saw me, she disappeared almost as soon as she appeared. After all this time I have got used to being on my own, locked away from society, as the night draws in, my mind now full of the possibilities and questions. My mind made up that if I see her the next day, I will swallow my pride and approach her, in disbelief that for me nothing has changed in the way

I think of her. Surely this must be the universe giving me a sign that my future is written and only for the better.

Quiet on the bus to work, the sound of the tyres on the road drowning out the constant chatter of my inmates, all excited for the day ahead and talk of what they will do to the missus when they finally get home. No-one notices my silence as we disembark, and my eyes avert to see her walking into the building. Dressed ready for a workout, chatting animatedly to her friends accompanying her. For me, she is special, the one woman that could change my life and my outlook. Just as I thought I could not catch her, she strides out of the changing rooms, towards the steam room. Speeding up my walk just enough so I can intercept her before she enters.

"Babes, I knew it was you," I said, trying to sound as non-committal and nonchalant as possible

"Hi, I thought it was you. Sorry, I have forgotten your name. What was it again?"

"You know my name. Stop being stupid. I didn't mean to stand you up. I got waylaid,"

She is cute when pissed off. I can almost see that bottom lip pouting in a sulk. Could grab her now and kiss it. Probably not the most useful thought at this moment as she tightens her towel around her,

her self-consciousness kicking in. How shy she can be is too endearing, but I can't stop laughing at her. "Babes, don't be angry. It couldn't be helped. It was totally out of my control,"

"You stood me up, and I've not heard from you in over 6 years. Then you stand in front of me like nothing happened. What could you have possibly been doing that stopped you from calling me? If you didn't want to see me, you should have just let me know."

She deserves to know the truth, a chance to be given an explanation

"I was arrested and have been in prison ever since. I am working here on day release. Meet me for a coffee at 4pm when I finish, and I will explain everything."

There she is already waiting for me by the time I get to the coffee shop. The bus won't be here for at least an hour, so at least we have plenty of time to get it all out in the open. She may never want to talk to me again. This is our last chance to work it out. Now or never. The conversation is simple, both obviously nervous. The subject wasn't important and damned if I could remember anything of what they said. This time together was precious, and it was to happen every evening while I worked at that gym. Every Tuesday night spent on the phone and open honest letters. Previous relationships have never been like this before. She allowed me to show my vulnerabilities, whilst feeling more like a man than ever before. There was never any judgement.

"You have a visitor," the guard announced. Strange as I'd not seen anyone in my whole time here. With trepidation, I walk to the visitation room, all the while pondering why she is here. I have not seen her since the day the raid happened. The conversation between us strained and unnatural. She wants to give it another go, allow my kids to get to know their father, but only if I move back in with her. My way of thinking was I would be a free man in all senses of the word, to explore this new me I have discovered. The reasons she gave have not convinced me of coming from a genuine place. I need to speak to the one that can help me make this decision. Her reaction to this news is a dreaded thought. Do I wait for our usual Tuesday call or grow some balls and just get it over with? Unusual for me to feel scared over telling women bad news. They have never really meant that much to me. After the honeymoon period, I'm usually gone or trying to get rid of them, otherwise it's too much hard work trying to maintain the relationship with my career.

"We need to talk. Without making you aware of the situation, I can't continue."

"I don't want to hear it," I said whilst holding back the tears.

"I just want to chat about the normal stuff. The bits that are just about you and me!"

"My ex has been to visit me this week. She wants me to move back in with her. I told her a one-bedroom flat organised, and that I needed to turn my life around. "

"But she hasn't come to see you the whole time you have been away. Never written or brought the kids to see you. Suddenly she wants you back?"

"I will not do it. I will plan with her to see the kids so I can get to know them properly. That's something I need to do!"

"This has to be the most heart-breaking thing I am ever going to say, but I think you need to give that relationship a go. It needs a chance. Your kids deserve to get to know their dad. Everything that has happened was because of you. It's not their fault. You have the paradox of choice, so I will help make it easier for you. Don't call me again!"

Every night at exactly 9.30pm I called her. She never answered, obviously trying to do the right thing. Sadness enveloped me in a way I didn't know was possible. I permanently engraved her image into my brain, never to be forgotten.

As darkness fell, it was a signal of some freedom to come away from the drudgery of daily home life. They threw everything that had happened into my face. There was no forgiveness or moving forwards. I was in hell. This was the true payment for my crimes. Time to hit the bars and maybe a club, allowing me to be myself and not live in a pretence. The music is loud, with the lights and fog making it difficult to see, but there she is, clear as day, coming down the stairs. Never have I seen her dressed up in make-up and fancy clothes. Think I like this side of her. Her tanned toned legs peeping out of the dress as she walks. As she strides towards me, the smile gets her attention. The last time I saw her this drunk, I had to rescue her and take her home. My priority is to protect her, drawing her to the corner of the room away from prying eyes. Happiness to see me is clear, or that could be the amount of alcohol she has consumed. Either way, I'm pleased that she is. If I was a public man, I could easily rip off that dress and devour her now.

Strange to think that we have never even kissed, and yet we remain emotionally entwined. Her touch making me squirm as perfectly manicured fingers creep down towards the zip of my jeans, opening with one swift movement and slides in to grip me. She doesn't move, just looks at me with longing. How I am resisting her is beyond me. I need to stop this, get her home to safety away from me. One more drink, sending her over the edge.

Seems we have come a full circle as I scoop her up and carry her to a taxi, resisting her advances as I take her home and to her door. To say goodbye was painful, knowing this would be the last time. I need to let her go. The driver pulls away as I watch her through the rear-view mirror, seeing her stand there feeling the same despair as myself.

Mr Mercedes Two

My heart broken, filled with ice, I take a more pragmatic approach to my dating journey. They must meet certain requirements. The list is extensive. No longer looking for love, but a companion. I don't need the excitement of the thrill of falling in love. It's needs to be more of a business arrangement. I am preparing for a life full of dullness and shite sex. I created a new profile on as many apps as possible. Gone were the pictures full of friends and vibrancy, replaced with bog standard everyday things. I had finally become a basic bitch.

Will I ever fall in love again, or do I just need to make a list of requirements and settle for whatever I can get? Sometimes I think this is what my friends have done so as not to be alone. I am happy to be in my company, but I'm not getting any younger, so it might be time to re-evaluate my approach. Sex, that is the main thing I'm missing. I should enjoy it now that my periods are in my distant past alongside wrinkle free skin, all night raves and ecstasy tablets. The journey of swiping has once more begun. It's a murky world and more difficult to navigate as I get older.

It coming to the end of autumn and I'm still unexplainably single! Before I wallow in self-pity and indulge in a box of soft centre chocolates and a bottle of whatever alcoholic scraps are still on offer in the gin cabinet, I ponder on whether to binge watch something on Netflix or peruse the wonders of Tinder. Obviously, the latter won. I'm a curious type. I'm hoping I've missed the end of the sales with just the dregs of society left on show.

Here he is! Mr Mercedes two. He couldn't be more different from the original one. Same job, same car, even the same part of town. That's where the similarities end. Nowhere near as good looking or funny. Definitely not as sexy, but my options are dwindling after wasting too much time pining for Mr Prisoner. He stands out from what is currently on offer for a couple of reasons. He is in good shape and still has a fine head of hair. Not the best style. But that's a minor point to quibble about. Very direct with his approach, like myself. He wants to get straight to the point and waste no time. There is no humour or a funny one liner. His interview technique stinks. We arranged a date within a couple of hours. I have nothing better to do and it sounds nice, what he has planned. A long walk around the local reservoir and beauty spot in the middle of autumn. Means no need to dress up, big coat, boots and jeans followed by a full English. Perfect for my low effort mood.

We talked back and forth for a few days, and the conversation wasn't something I would call enlightening. Mainly the conversation was inexplicably about the benefits of different disinfectants on sale and went through his daily routine of cleanliness. It's not exactly riveting stuff, and never did I think I would sink this low in my desperation to find a partner. His obsession, worse than I originally thought. Was I this desperate to have a partner that I was now willing to endure a life of constant cleaning and the excitement of shopping trips left to the local discount store? Where is the adventure, ticking off the bucket list together, growing old disgracefully and the creation of memories as our golden years approach? I've exhausted all possibilities with limited options on show.

Now that we have agreed on a date and venue, I can't back out. The thought of standing him or cancelling doesn't cross my mind. I will just have to grin and bear it and hope I am pleasantly surprised. Positivity is the mindset I need to keep.

The day has arrived, handpicking my outfit. Still needs to be a stylish walk, even if it is freezing outside. A scarlet red parka, with jeans and my brand-new white hi tops. Of course, I get lost on the way, much to his exasperation. The way he talks to me on the car phone is demeaning, his voice full of disdain at my sheer stupidity. Truth of the matter is he hadn't given me an exact location. The drive becoming stressful; I pull into a side street, park up, and tell him to come and get me. Within five minutes, I see him waving as though he was guiding a jumbo jet onto the runway. Deep breath in preparation, I lock up the car and go towards him as he moves to his car. I wasn't sure where he worked, but his vehicle was the same as Mr Mercedes. Upon sight, the memories flow back, and a smile sneaks out of my lips. The drive into the hills wasn't as bad as I thought it would be. He is being friendly and tells a joke or two, not the type you have to hold your stomach and the giggles turn in to full on snorting, but it's a good start.

The dreaded question comes, but I can't help asking it.

"How has Tinder been treating you? " I said in my usual careless fashion. This question only gets asked once I have discovered we have nothing in common to talk about.

"I've had a few dates, not met anyone I wanted to take on a second date, though. Went for dinner with one. She turned up in a red coat, put me off straight away. I'm not a fan of colour."

It took me a few moments to realise what he said as I nervously clutch my brand new specially purchased for the date bright red coat. Pulling it around me to ensure a cosy, secure feeling. Was he joking, trying to get a bit of banter going? His face told me otherwise. He was deadly serious. As he drives, I wonder if I would die if I jumped out of his car into oncoming traffic. Seemed like a viable option, which I was seriously considering. Trapped in my second to worst nightmare, coming a close to my first, which would be running to escape being eaten alive by an army of zombies. The saving grace was the local beauty spot, that even on this bitter day with grey skies, welcomed the influx of visitors ready to soak up the peaceful surrounding. He opens the boot of his car to take out hiking boots, whilst taking a gander at my brilliant white trainers.

"Do you have any walking boots with you?" he said in a tone dripping with disbelief at my choice of footwear. "What size shoes are you?"

"Size five," I said defensively.

"Oh, I would have let you borrow a pair of mine, but I'm a size four. "

That's it! I'm done! We all know what they say about the size of feet. The rest of the day, I am now picturing some sort of micro penis. I can't get the image out of my head. Not that I was looking at this guy sexually in any shape or form. But it's there now, it's refusing to move from my head, and we still have the walk to do. All I can do is make the best of an unpleasant situation, put a brave face on and smile, joke my way through it. As we start the trek around the reservoir, all unfamiliar territory for me, he decides on the route we will take. Now if I was a bad minded person, I would say he picked the muddiest route on purpose. Feet stuck a few times as they squelched in the quicksand puddles. My squeals of laughter were becoming an irritant to him. I knew I was annoying him, but I didn't care. He's got size four feet, for fuck's sake. They wouldn't even make a ripple in the shallow, wet depth of his mind. I took the morning of work to enjoy myself, and that was exactly what I intend to do. Pushing harder for conversation, I ask about his work. Much to my surprise, he works in the same sales showroom as my other Mr Mercedes. I revel in telling him about my friend that works with him, minus a lot of the details of our encounters. A storm clouds his face, obvious anger displayed, with a fight to hide his expressions. He obviously knows how his higher superior competitor behaves with the fairer sex online. This guy is not even in the same class.

We move onto our family lives; asking if I have kids. A brownie point earned. I love to talk and boast about how wonderful my kids are. Even their smallest of achievements and fails and for a first date to be asking is special to me. Maybe he is interested in me. I saw him trying to check out the bum earlier as I strode ahead of him, finally relaxing and feel comfortable in his presence. He must warm to me, see my potential as a future, but could I see the potential in him? He became quieter as I talked about the kids. The slight sliver of hope for anything between was dwindling away into the ether. As we walk back to the car, it was further than walking the green mile with the same amount of dread. Feet heavy at the bottom of my legs. Just another disappointment to add to the ever-expanding list.

As we make our way to the car, we pass an older gentleman looking dapper in his flat cap and scarf, enjoying his surroundings, minding his own business. He greets us with a friendly smile, calls his playful dog over. Ignoring him, the dog takes a massive shit just in front of Mr Mercedes 2. Personally, I think this is hilarious, but for him, you would think chemical warfare had just been announced and he needed to protect his territory.

"Hope you are going to clean that up. It's disgusting letting your dog shit in the grass." He snaps to the bemused man. "I bet your house smells of shit. Can't stand people like you!"

Please let a tsunami take over the reservoir and sweep me up at this very moment. Passers-by are staring at us. Mr Mercedes 2 is fuming, his ferret like face swelling into a beetroot.

"Why would you do that?" I hiss through pursed lips. "He's just an old man enjoying the fresh air with his dog. For all you know, that could be his only companion in life."

"He should pick it up straight away. It's not right, a kid could walk on that grass!"

"You didn't exactly give him a chance. You could still see the steam coming off it. Look at him, he's getting the poo bags out of his pocket."

The guy is moving slowly, exasperated with his zip, refusing to budge. A twang of compassion overcomes me as I approach him to apologise and help him gain his compassion and collect his dogs' deposits for him. Greeted with a thank you and a smile, all I can think is - if only you were 25 years younger? You are a lot nicer than the prick I mistakenly agreed to meet. I turn sharply and march ahead towards his pristine car. Wishing I was a bitch, I could take off my once white trainers, now looking like they had played a thousand football games during a rainstorm and wipe them all over the vehicle. By the time he makes it back to me, I've been to the bathrooms to clean up and give my hands a good scrub.

"So, are you going to tell me what that was all about?

"You have kids. I don't want any yet or want a woman who does!"

"Don't you think that would have been a question to ask before you asked me out on a date? Surely if that was a deal breaker for you, it would have been good to bring it up first. You have just wasted both our times."

"Is that how you feel? That it was a waste of your time coming here. You don't understand. Everything in my house is white, the floors, the walls, the furniture. I don't want kids in there making it messy. I spend 4 hours a day cleaning."

"You have serious issues, and I would like to be taken back to my car now."

"You are not getting in my car with those shoes on. They are too dirty!"

"Fuck you" as I flip him the bird and off I go.

Contemplating the 5 mile walk back to my car, I am not spending a minute longer with this man than needs be. Two hours later, I arrive at my car once I remembered where it was. What a disaster. My feet are killing me and all I want to do is pee myself. Squirming in my seat all the way home. Dancing on the doorstep as I try to get the key to work, all the while my bladder is reminding me of the urgency. Dash to the toilet. Relief is bliss as I remind myself that he only has a size four feet. Lucky escape if you ask me!

Mr Mercedes 2 says...

What can I say? This is one woman who needs to grow up and get some sessions with an anger management counsellor. She started off well, and there is no denying she is a good looking. A vague sense of familiarity hits me when I see her profile. I know her from somewhere, but I'm sure we have never met. She is funny, even if her humour is different to mine as she seems to laugh at everything. Does she take anything seriously? One good thing we have in common is our love of disinfectants for the home. My favourite is clean linen. Each night before I go to bed, I get all my dishcloths and soak them in the sink, then the house smells lovely, and I can do a quick one hour clean before I head off to work. I love my home with it clean white lines and mirrored furniture. The light bounces around the room to make mini rainbows. Any woman who wants to be part of my life needs to understand that she will have to be prepared to take part in my cleaning ritual. The last one had to go, after placing her coffee mug on my mirrored table, leaving a mark. A lovely woman, but that is just scruffy for me. People should have more pride in themselves. Before I leave the house, I sanitised every light switch I touch, leave the cleaning supplies in a little cupboard by the front door so it is there when I come home to clean again before I touch them. The same with the car and at work. My colleagues make jokes about it, it just means they wish they could have my discipline. Water of a duck's back.

One guy who gets me as he is just as disciplined as I with his fitness journey. Chatting in the staff canteen, I open up to him about being single, about the struggle to find a woman who can live up to my high expectations. His tales of his online dating adventures have me in shock and amazement. Not sure I could sleep with that many, though. The thought of all those bodily fluids is making me queasy. How much would my bills go up because of the washing machine constantly cleaning bedding? Together, he helps me build a profile, taking some quick selfies around the showroom. I have a very particular taste. They must look well groomed, smart, intelligent and free of any baggage.

Every lunch time we meet, to discuss our progress and share stories. He seems to have it easier than me. He clicks his fingers and the ladies come running. Where am I going wrong? Just the other day he disappeared at lunchtime, came back flushed and content, with tales of his visit to a regular lady he sees. Describing their first proper date, which ended with them having sex in the back of his car in the middle of a graveyard. Sounds like something out of a porn film, obviously has no respect for herself. Not for me, that type of woman. The date I have tomorrow is questionable. She has all the right attributes, but something is niggling me in the back of my mind. The familiarity, the sense of knowing, could be the reason I asked her to meet me. Hope she doesn't turn up in a red coat. They all seem to own one which repels me. It screams, attention grabbing. Look at me, I'm here. A nice classic black jacket or Crombie is stylish. Sensible shoes are also a must. Easy to clean and suitable for the task at hand.

The morning comes in cold, time to wrap up warm for my ideal date. A walk around the local reservoir followed by a full English breakfast with all the trimmings, tea, and toast. Driving towards the location, the realisation that we haven't arranged a meeting point dawns on me. Not the best start, but

I am sure if we mean it to be, it will just naturally happen. The alert of a phone call takes me out of autopilot as I can hear a distressed voice on the other end. She's lost. My eyes roll so far back, they give me pain in the sockets. I thought she was the independent type and already she is asking for me to help her and come to her aid. The last thing I need is a partner who needs looking after. Regardless of the fact we had no set location, she should be able to use her wits to guide her to the correct place. I signal that I have found by waving both arms. Making her way towards me, my worst fears confirmed. She has on a red parka, not only is she ditsy, but an attention seeker. No doubt about it, I'm an excellent judge of character and I have made my decision on her instantly. This will not go any further than today, not even a breakfast, which irks me. I was looking forward to that. Her only redeeming quality is that she looks like pictures, unlike most of them, full of Botox and filters.

Incessant chatting about absolutely nothing during the drive. Her voice is grating on me, at the same level of fingers scraping a blackboard.

The reservoir is stunning today. Even through the grey clouds, the sun is trying to break through with limited will to shine. She is trying to make conversation, asking questions to get to know me. Maybe I have misjudged her and should give her a chance. The subject of where I work comes up and now it all makes sense why she seemed so familiar. She is, in fact, Miss Graveyard. I feel duped by her lies of wanting a relationship and a partner to enjoy and share life with. Why not just be honest and admit you are after casual sex? I'm doing well keeping a lid on my anger. Now she tells me she has three kids, one who will need care for the rest of his life. I do not want a woman with kids. Feeling like her deception has blindsided me, my anger further increases when a big daft Labrador bounds over to me and does a massive shit at my feet. With the irritant laughing uncontrollably, I lose my temper on its owner. A dapper old gent minding his own business while attempting to control his animal. I will never understand why people want pets, filthy, dirty beings that smell of dust and mould. Major rules in my house are no pets or kids. It's not much to ask for!

Now she has ran over to the gentleman to help him with the audacity to apologise on my behalf, before marching off back to the car. I can't remember half the crap she came out with, but a genuine lady wouldn't talk to that. And how dare she raise her voice to me? Finally catching up to her at the car, with her muddy trainers. I feel no guilt that she has completely ruined her expensive shoes. It is her own fault she made a stupid decision to wear them.

"You are going to have to take them off before you get in. I can't have dirt spreading over my car."

"Fuck you" while giving me the middle finger in a tantrum, she storms off to walk back to her own car

More confirmation that there is no future between us. The thought of introducing her to family and friends already makes me feel embarrassed. One thing you can say about this girl is that she is stubborn. As I drive past her already halfway down the road, I almost stop to get her in the car, deciding not to after the way she spoke to me. Anger management issues, I'll text her my counsellor's number!

Mr Micro Penis

What a disaster my last date turned out to be. Can I really carry on with this online dating malarkey? I am now classified as a serial dater. What will this mean for my future? Forever single, with a growing despondency towards the men I meet. Another wedding invitation falling onto the doormat with no plus one. All my friends have given up on me ever finding love. A decision already made for me. Have they forgotten how tenacious I am? Part of me thinks they keep inviting me to rub it into my face and gloat about their agreement to marry men I would think as substandard. I tried dating down, obviously didn't work.

I need to find a date for this next wedding. There is not a chance that I am going on my own to another one. He needs to be handsome, rich, the body of an Adonis with a stellar personality. Just so my friends can see, they may have bolted before the gate has closed. Opted for the lesser and gone bargain basement shopping. Fooling myself into this belief is the only thing that is keeping me going through this journey. My dating life compared to off roading with broken suspension. Dangerous, exciting, but will end up with a good dose of whiplash, while avoiding all those red flags.

A new conversation has started. He is not amazing looking, but has a sexy swagger about him. The profile was questionable, just a torso for his major picture and what a torso it was. It needed more investigation, to dig a little deeper into the six-pack. The hint of what could be below the bottom of the waistband of the underpants showing, allowing my imagination to be titillated. My illusions are about to be shattered as the dreaded whistle of a notification disturbs my session of self-love and gratification. Terrible timing, killing the moment as the ecstasy of climax was at its pinnacle. To be continued ...

Now my attention is now diverted, he best be able to keep hold of it and take full advantage. Please don't bore me, imploring to the dating gods to give me a good one that will stick. The goal posts always changing, ever hopeful that this is he. The smiles and laughter he brings makes more appealing as the days pass. Somehow, I have found someone who can hold a normal conversation while also littered with double entendres, sending us both into fits of giggles. We talk for a couple of weeks before we finally agree to meet. That he hasn't tried to rush me is a plus, progressing organically to a sexual conversation. What is it with men? They must impress upon you the size of their penis. Sounds impressive, but being a realist, I minus a couple of centimetres. Unlike most blokes that boast about the quality of their nether regions, itching to show it off as a dick pic, he hasn't sent me one, which is another plus point. I am taking it as he is being respectful, and the sexting is harmless flirting between two grown adults.

Because of previous experiences, I didn't want to get ahead of myself and build the excitement around this. Letting him take charge, I allowed him to arrange the date. He wanted to go to a popular nightclub in town that he regularly visited. First red flag that I ignored, thinking it was pinker. Ask me this twenty years ago, I would have been all over it, but nowadays I need a bit more sophistication. Shouting into someone's ear, just so they can mishear me would not be my ideal date. Give him a second chance to remedy this, my head tells me. My heart has always misguided me. Now is the time to stop listening. It worries me that a fifty-year-old man is still hanging out in a nightclub that is renowned for hot young girls, trying to grab her older money man. Reservations are creeping in.

Thankfully, he has changed the date to one of the nicest hotel restaurants in town. I know he has booked a room as well. It makes sense as he lives a couple of hours away. I want him to be a to relax as we get to know each other without checking his watch.

Wearing my favourite sexy little black dress and heels, showing the firmness of my thighs when I walk, to see him sitting cross-legged, dressed in a tweed jacket, checking his phone. I stand before him, waiting for him to look up and notice me. With a determined slowness, he smiles and offers me a drink. We are getting along well. As I relax being in his company, I can feel myself melt into the soft leather sofa he has chosen for us in a darker corner of the bar. The evening is balmy, as we venture outside for a cigarette, which makes little sense, as I only smoke when under the influence of a lot of alcohol. I've only had one vodka, lime and lemonade. Must be nerves getting to me, although I feel completely rational. I have not felt this comfortable in the company of a new man in a long time. A bit too relaxed, as he went in for the kiss, which I accepted with eager passion. This guy has got skills, just the right amount of tenderness with the urgency of his needs. Thankful that he didn't treat my face as a washing machine.

We move to his hotel room for the dinner he has ordered. In normal circumstances, I would never have done this, but he explains the hotel has a private dining facility and true to his word, when we enter, a butler greets us with a fully laid dining table, complete with a single stem rose vase, cloches to keep the food warm and champagne on ice. Politely, I refuse the champagne with my first date rules; I have a two-drink limit; the bubbles go straight to my head, and I need to stay lucid. The room is already spinning a little, so I am grateful when he pulls out my chair, inviting me to sit. I gratefully accept the offer of sparkling water. As the butler pours, he asks me if I am ok, if I need any help. Strange thing to ask, I came here under no duress. Dinner is beautiful, a medium rare steak Diane, served with a garlic mash and greens. Oh shit, I need the bathroom. Think I am going to vomit. Queasy and overheating, I can't decide if it's a hot flush or I need to empty the contents of my stomach into the porcelain bowl. Now we are alone with the butler left and dinner cleared away. I excuse myself. Hot damn! I've only seen this bathroom in glossy magazines outside of my meagre budget. The shower could fit a large family or a complete orgy if you felt inclined. Deep black tiles, sharp gold waterfall taps trimming the freestanding bath, with a television embedded into the wall. Panic over, no need to throw up, just overheating as seems to have become the norm. A glance in the mirror showing a face of melted make-up. I freshen up and make my way back into the suite. It did not prepare me for the visual atrocity was to greet my eyes.

At first, sneaking a peek through the slit of the bathroom door, I see the beautiful torso that had first pulled me in. Thoughts running through my mind of the stoking and licking to lines showing his perfected abs. I gather myself to gain the willpower to say no. New rule! No sex on the first date! Tempting as it may be, I must learn to behave myself in life. Tonight is the night I turn a corner and resist temptation. Boldy, flinging open the door full of determination. As he hears my entrance, he flings his knees up to his shoulders. Displaying his carefully manicured anal passage that he forgot to clean properly after his last visit to the toilet.

"Lick my arse!" he said with limited breath capacity as his body now folded in half.
"Excuse me? I missed that last statement. Did you just say what I think you said?"

"Yes, lick my arse now! Then I will show you the time of your life!"

Trying to avert my eyes from the abomination before me, finding anywhere else to focus, I become drawn to the two pairs of balled up socks on the floor. There is only one reason men would need this accessory: the same reason women needed the Wonderbra in the nineties! To push, fill, and enlarge. I am taken over by curiosity now. As hard as I try not to look, my subconsciousness takes over. The involuntary movement of my eyes towards his groin confirms his masculine boasts of being well endowed was just a figment of his imagination. Fascination also taken over, doing my best not to stare as I've never come across a micro penis in my life while also still repelled at the chocolate starfish still confronting me, begging for my tongue to play with it.

"I've got to go. Got an early start in the morning." I said, while trying to gather my composure and belongings. Sea legs kicking in as the floor feels as though a tsunami was about to hit. I attempt to gracefully back out of the door. Once in the elevator, not fully understanding what has happened, the full enormity of my lack of sobriety hits me. Stumbling into the foyer of the hotel, I see the friendly face of the bartender as he catches me.

"You OK love? I knew I was right to refuse him that last triple vodka. Let me call you a cab and get you home safely."

Mr Micro Penis says...

Born with a less than average penis, growing up with bullying, and forever told that I was deformed, knocked my confidence. That was until I fell in love with an amazing creature. We stayed together for twenty years, both virgins when we met in our teenage years. Neither knowing anything different, knowing our sex life would never be standard. We had to be adventurous and think out of the box. Over the years, we discovered many ways to pleasure each other to bring satisfaction. She was so understanding of my needs and what I could bring to the relationship outside the bedroom that my miniscule appendage didn't matter to her. Our journey together led us to realise we both developed a love of anal play and rimming. It was no longer considering a strange kink by the world, thanks to the easy access to porn and the birth of the internet. If I close my eyes, I can take myself back to a place filled with love, affection, and the feel of her probing, wet tongue deep into my back passage. As much as I would try, I could never hold back with the screams of intensity falling in time with my orgasm. Together, we were perfect in every way. As we got older, the subject of children came up several times. Her need to reproduce would overcome her desire for me. I loved her so much that I had to let her go. The physical inability to help her get pregnant caused the start of our relationship falling apart.

To get over losing the one woman I would always love, I hit the clubs in the city centre, developing a taste for the younger ladies looking for a sugar daddy. They were not too bothered by having regular sex. If I paid for their shopping in the designer stores, kept their champagne glasses topped up, they would occasionally indulge in my anal games. The soulless agreements never filled the void for the emotional engagement I craved. My soul mate was now gone from life, after Facebook stalking, happy with her new man and baby. I needed to do the same and find a new person to share my life with.

Just because I have a small penis, doesn't mean I don't have the same libido, sexual desires, and emotional needs as any other man. I am just different, and it's our differences that make the world a beautiful place. But I do struggle to get an erection and have a low sperm count. It was something my parents never really talked about, my dad, especially as he saw it as a reflection of his own masculinity. No-one thought to investigate it medically, although I have done my research online. It's a condition called Hypospadias. In all honesty, I'm thankful my parents never wanted to investigate why I was born with a micro penis. In the sixties and seventies, they would put you through sex reassignment. Thankfully, this no longer happens. The hardest part, excuse the pun, is trying to find a woman who is happy with it. She has to be very open-minded and a lot adventurous in the bedroom department. These women are few and far between. It's not exactly something you tell people when you first meet, so I don't. I let them discover for themselves, usually after lots of foreplay, and I've given her the best orgasm of her life.

Online, I try to come across cocky and I always tell them I'm well endowed. Still unsure why I do this. I hope they will fall for my personality and not really care by the time we come to do the carnal deed. There is one that has caught my eye and kept my attention. She is funny, full of sarcasm and witty. Good looks and brains are sexy to me. For days we talk and eventually I bite the bullet and ask her out on a date. Somewhere classy is needed, and I have just the perfect place to take her. An exclusive hotel in town complete with a butler experience. At least that way, if we decide to sleep together, we are in the right place.

I wait patiently in the bar for her to arrive while nursing a bottle of non-alcoholic lager in my hands. With the knowledge of her favourite drink, I have one specially prepared. I know it's wrong, but I've ordered her a triple instead of a single. Help her relax and relieve any nerves she might have. A benefit of getting her into this state of mind. I am hoping she is one of those girls that feel horny after a few drinks. She has already informed that she has a two-drink rule on the first date with no sex. Too many mistakes made in the past that they do not prepare her to want to repeat. I've heard that before, but they all give in the end and pushing her boundaries just a little will be a good thing for her. She will grow as a human and as a woman. Once they let it go, they rarely notice my cock until it's too late. The flush of alcohol is showing on her face. A bit of fresh air would do her the world of good. The freshness of a cool summer evening feels good and presents the opportunity for me to be a gentleman. As I wrap my tweed jacket around her shoulders, I place a soft kiss on her lips to test her response. She smells so good. I step up the intensity which is matched by her.

"Come on, let's get back inside for one more drink before dinner." I said while taking her by the hand and leading her back to the soft leather sofa in the cosy corner of the bar I selected for us. "You are an amazing kisser. I have got a feeling we are going to get along fine."

I pick up her triple vodka and my alcohol-free beer to escort her to dinner. She is going to be blown away by what is in store for us. A personal butler served her favourite foods in luxury. No distractions, just us two in the best suite in the hotel. I've pulled out all the stops. Despite it not being the cheapest date I have ever been on; a good impression has to be made as I have high expectations of this female. She is open and honest, with a broad mind. She is going to need it. Images of her naked, wearing a strap on, give me a hard on. One benefit of being in the small department is that no-one can see this, plus it is hiding behind the two pairs of designer socks I have tucked into my briefs.

She refuses the Champagne offered to her, selecting a sparkling water instead. I thought she was just trying to appear as a good girl and of high moral standard when the two drinks rule was enforced. Unbeknown to her, she is way past that limit. Had to be on at least 6 shots. Come to think about it, she was a little unsteady on her feet and, after dinner, looked very pale. Making her excuses, she departs to the bathroom, turning a funny shade of green. Maybe I have gone too far with the extra shots in her drinks, even after telling me she is a lightweight. Dismissing the butler and clearing the room of all the evidence of the romantic dinner, the sound of the water hitting the metal sink signals she will be back in the room feeling fresher and ready to take our relationship to the next level.

As I hurry to strip down and lay seductively on the bed to surprise her, the bathroom door opens ajar to allow a stripe of light onto the bedroom, adding a sheen onto my torso fighting against the moonlight coming through the windows. The door quickly closes as she retreats into the bathroom. What is going through her mind? Maybe it's all too much for her to handle. She can't get over her luck at how sexy I am. I see this as a positive sign she is making the final preparations ready for me. Not reading the room, the biggest error of judgement I have made in a long time happens. While waiting for her to reappear, a full porn reel runs through my mind with her as the star, strap on attached, ready to give me a good pegging. Swapping between the appendage and the flick of her tongue, probing my posterior entrance. Lost in the moment, I pull my knees up to my shoulders as she enters the room to give her a full view of the goods to entice her into my world.

"Lick my arse," I said throatily, feeling the pressure of being bent in half in my lungs.

"Excuse me? Did you just say want I think you did?"

"Yes, lick my arse and I'll give you the time of your life!"

At that moment, reality kicks in. How have I misjudged this situation so badly? Retreating with a drunken stagger from the room, leaving me to reflect on my behaviour. I have never heard from her since, which is a damn shame. It's her loss. She obviously doesn't realise when she was at a precipice to the end of her dating life. Back to Tinder for me

Maria R Peter

The Dick Pic!

Before we look at the weird and wonderful realm of the unsolicited dick pic, I want to say that there are women out there that are just as guilty of this. I have been told by many of my male acquaintances, who have received what I can only commonly term as the pussy pic! But I write this book from a straight female perspective, so dick pic it is!

The dick pic can bring up a range of emotions that most of us want to deny. Yes, we sit there publicly and shout about our disgust and violation of our eyes. But there is a strange fascination with them. Before I embarked on my dating adventures, it had been a while since I had seen a male body, so there was a strange titillation that was happening. It woke me to realise I was still a sexual being. I haven't seen many dicks in my lifetime, but the variety was insane! All shapes and sizes were flying into my inbox. If I ignored them, they would find another route to send it. Usually through the disappearing message function on Instagram.

I didn't read the signs that one was coming in my direction. I was still new to this online dating malarkey. Why do they keep sending me an aubergine emoji? It makes little sense!

The matches were happening, the exchange of WhatsApp numbers (I have a different one to my personal number and the block function is a godsend) and thus the flurry of dick pics. Do not think all dick pics are equal. I got so many at one point; we set a WhatsApp group up called Cock of the week. I feel no shame in this. My girls needed the update of what was happening in my dating story. Why was I becoming disillusioned?

Not all dick pics are the same!

I have had hundreds, so we are just going to talk about a few.

The ten seconders!

No, it is not what you think, ladies. Take your minds out of the gutter!

This is a special breed and shows the arrogance of the male behind the picture. A good-looking man, who usually chats on a Sunday morning while still lay in bed. Undoubtably, having had no success on a Saturday night in the clubs, he is up for a bit of hanky panky with anyone who will take it. How could a girl refuse? This lady could, that's for sure.

So, he charms you, makes you feel as though you are the one and only he is talking to on Tinder. You cave in and give him your digits. Within 10 seconds of those digits being handed over, voilà! The dick pic has arrived. Full naked frontal standing in his doorway like the Leonardo Da Vinci Vitruvian Man! Oh My! That was fast work. But going with the picture was his address! What? Am I meant to feel compelled to drop everything on my lazy Sunday, run around, find a babysitter, and see if there is anything resembling lingerie in my big knicker drawer?

Hit you from all angles!

Another strange phenomenon, to receive not one but ten pics in one go. From every angle possible. Is this man a contortionist? This could interest! But no, it's not. It doesn't photograph well from the first angle, so maybe he needed the backup plan. Persuasion, maybe? Bit like a profile picture. You know your best angles. My response. "You best get to the doctor, mate; I can see an unexplained rash there!" I received no more from him, and I hope he booked a date at his local GUM clinic.

Maria R Peter

The Masturbator!

This is a regular occurrence. Damn you, video calling.

Masturbator one. (Yes, there have been more than a few). This is the guy who has filmed himself and sent to as many women as humanly possible. A quick one-minute video of when he is nearly complete. But with a random girl's name. This affronted me and I called him out at once. He had not said my name. How dare he send me a video and it was not even about me! He went away for 5 minutes, yes that's right ladies, 5 minutes and sent me another one with him repeating my name, like I was the only one for him and on his mind constantly. The romance was too much! BLOCKED!

Masturbator two. The wife does not understand me type of male. Men, let me tell you, this has never been sexy and never will be! Sneaking into the downstairs toilet of their house, while kids and missus are asleep upstairs and then they send their performance to you! Only way to put it politely. BLOCKED!

Masturbator three. The public one! You find yourself sat comfortably with friends, having a drink, enjoying your evening. The drinks are flowing, and the laughter is loud. Usually from the stories of my dating life, with my friends looking on at me in both pity and amusement. Suddenly, the video calling goes. Your every instinct is telling you not to answer, but you do anyway. And there he is in all his glory, showing you his one-handed skills. Until you scan the phone around the room so he can see you are with company. Funny enough, he hangs up! Blocked so many times, but keeps creating new accounts to get in touch, but thankfully the video calls have ended.

So, the moral of the story is, if you have received a dick pic, he has sent it to every woman who caved in and exchanged numbers. Do not feel bad if you've never had one. Be thankful, be grateful. It is a sign of respect, and you are talking to the right sort of men. Unlike myself!

Mr Ex

Staring at the cold cappuccino on the rickety wooden table next to the window in a grubby café as I reflect on the sadness of my life. I need time out, a breakaway from everything. My work is sparse currently, so now the timing is perfect to get away from it all. Checking my diary, there is nothing booked in for a couple of months' time, blocking out seven days and a mental note to get on the travel websites for a last-minute break. Somewhere cool where I get the benefits of beach and city. As I dream of all the amazing places I could visit and never had the chance to check out while I was with the ex, I hear a rapping on the window. For fuck's sake! It's him. His uncanny ability to appear as soon as I think of moving forward with my life, as though to remind me he will always have control of me. Just his presence in my near vicinity rattles my nerves and I can't help but be transported back to those years with him.

It's 2am, the baby is finally asleep. The bed welcoming me to dive under the feather duvet and wrap myself in its comfort. As I feel my eyes finally succumbing to sleep, I hear the key turn in the lock of the front door. Drunken steps banging up the stairs towards our bedroom. I turn away from the door, pretending that I am already in slumber in the sheer hope that he will just look in and go away. The events of the next five minutes are so predictable. His fist connecting with my face with such force, the blood drips down my cheek until I gain the metal taste on my lips.

"You slag! Who are you fucking now?" he said with pure conviction. He really believes that I have the time to get up and find someone else to fuck. Not only have I got a business to run, but I have a child who sleeps for three to hours every night, maximum. I'm too scared to leave the house and rarely talk to my friends or go on social media. Part of me thinks its guilt transference

The stench of a brewery on his being surrounding my senses. I am becoming claustrophobic and have no time for a panic attack. It's fight or flight. I have been through this so many times. It's the same drill over and over again. Groundhog Day on the calendar. I hold back the tears and yelps of pain. Just stay still and he will stop. That is the usual pattern. There is something different about tonight. Something must have gone wrong at work, as he is determined to take his issues out on me. I fear for what is coming when I feel myself up in the air and flying across the room, landing on the dressing table with bottles and glass from the mirror raining down upon me. Shards and splinters, sticking into my skin as he comes towards me. Paralysed with fear, knowing full well I should kick him in the balls and do a runner, I just stare at him. Willing him to come for me and get it all over with. Not caring if this is the moment, he kills me, and I'm gone forever. His enormous hands squeezing around my neck as he flips me over, pulls down my shorts and enters me from behind. The violence, aggression and hatred in every push, no care of the hurt and humiliation he is putting me through. As he removes himself from inside of me, he sharply pulls my hair back, so I am facing his dick and comes all over me. Finalising the insult, collects his saliva to spit in my face. Finally, he lets go as I drop to the floor. Exhausted.

"Look at you! You are a gross slag. Can't believe I have a fat girlfriend who is not even a wonderful mother!"

He leaves the room with pure disgust for me apparent his face, punching the wall on the way out. I make my way to the bathroom, too scared to look at the damage in the mirror. Searching for my tweezers to remove the glass embedded in my skin. Still shaking from the assault, tears streaming down my face as I swab the cuts and bruising that are going to appear in the morning. This is the last time he is doing this to me. I need to make that call and get out of here. At least if he is taking it out on me, then he will leave the kids alone.

Two months later, in the middle of the night, the van of a friend, packed with the essentials. The kids' beds, clothes and toys. I have just a small suitcase of my own and we go. Off starting a new and better life.

His voice is behind me, bring me out of my memories, checking my surrounding and now cold cup of coffee

He asks, "Why are you ignoring me?"

"I'm not. I just didn't see you. Sorry I can't stop and chat. I've got an appointment to get to."

I've always found it easier to just make up an excuse to get out of there, rather than enter a discussion with him. It only ever goes one way, and that is into an argument. This happens less frequently, as I no longer fear him and always argue back. I am finally free of his clutches. One day, he will wake up and come to the same conclusion.

Mr Ex says...

Mr Ex was given no right to reply!

Mr Rebound

Holiday booked for the end of summer. Off to the Emerald Isle for a week. The best friend talked into coming with me. She wanted a week in Tenerife, but Ireland is always somewhere I have wanted to go. I'm paying, so I get to decide. A few days in Dublin, Galway and County Cavan. Hire a car and explore with freedom. Having this to look forward to hasn't stopped me still searching online for what seems to be an empty shallow quest. The entire world has been lying to me saying that online dating works. That elusive partner I speak of is just an enigma. I hear about them all the time, but do they ever appear? Where is my holy grail? The promise of eternal love? I jump from one disaster to another.

He looks cute, non-threatening. Complete opposite of my usual selections. I have found him on an app, or rather he found me, where they can message me directly without matching. Strange messages coming my way. Not one good opening line. There was a guy who has a profile picture of a set of stairs. I'm bamboozled, think I'll stick with the cute one for my next adventure. We have a few mutual acquaintances, as he is a dance teacher.

Never dated a dancer before, always like to keep my love life separate from my work life. As I am now retired from that profession, it should be OK. My fingers crossed that I could have turned a corner and picked someone half decent.

One night of talking and the energy between us is amazing. I can't decide if it is a friendship one or something romantic could bubble away under the ether and turn in to hot lava of a volcanic eruption. We are getting along so well; we switch over to video calling. Talking into the early hours of the morning, our passion for dance the common denominator.

Fast forward a week and here I am meeting him in the local park. All I need is twenty fags, a bottle of cider and take over the swings, not allowing the kids to play on them, and I could be transported back to my teenage dating experiences. There is a nip in the air and I'm regretting just wearing my leather biker jacket. He's wrapped up warm in a knee-length bubble jacket. Nice and cosy. He could sit here all day and not feel the chill.

"Let us walk. This park has a path that connects to the country park. It's much prettier." I say with a determination to get warm. That's the problem with this country. You can never rely on the weather. We reach the small café and order a latte for me and a hot chocolate, complete with sprinkles and marshmallows for him. He walks with a funny gait and seems to skip. I must imagine it. There is no way I'm on a date with a fifty-year-old man who skips along through his day while drinking kiddie beverages. Attracted to the play area again, we end up sitting in the sandpit with a boisterous toddler throwing sand in our direction, much to my annoyance. He jumps up excitedly after seeing a solitary log, climbing onto it and starts dancing. "Let's do the dirty dancing moves. C'mon, it's fun." he says.

Full of glee and wonderment. Has he never seen a log before? Am I on a play date and forgot to bring the children? He is sweet enough, seems kind and gentle. Even if he is from another planet. I'm too cold to even enjoy his immaturity. He is having a great time. Living his best life, meanwhile I am just getting more and more grumpy. I'm cold and hungry. I just want to go home and curl up on the sofa.

"Do you fancy pizza and a movie? We will go to my house and order one in." I say. Part of me wishes he will politely decline and be on his way. Fuck me, he agrees, jumping about as if the Easter bunny possessed him. Movie night it is then! I've got nothing better to do and would only go home to an empty house. Berating myself on the drive home as he follows me in my car. One positive, I must move out of my comfort zone as I would never invite a relative stranger to my home. This is my sacred sanctuary. Few get through the front door. If I had a choice, I wouldn't even let the kids in.

Pizza ordered. Dash to the toilet to relieve to my ever-complaining bladder with thoughts of dread at knowing purchases of incontinence pads looms closer. Being the cordial host that I am, I let him select the movie. Fingers crossed he doesn't pick a Star Wars, Marvel, or something similar. I'm fucked. He picks some superhero nonsense; I am officially on a date with a teenage boy under the guise of a grown man. Only one solution to get me through this. Curl up on the sofa, head on his lap and fall asleep. Best idea I've had in eons. In two hours, I can wake up and pretend I've loved his company.

I awake just before the ending to see him completely engrossed in the movie. Probably hasn't even noticed my absence through the power of slumber or he was just thankful for my silence and pizza. The offer of coffee declined; he wants a cola. Dutifully, I go to the kitchen to prepare his drink, on the hunt for one of my sons drinking cups. Found it!

Dancing Santas with a twirly straw. "That cup is ace. Really cool." he says with no irony. "Glad you like it! I've enjoyed your company this evening. Maybe we could chat and get to know each other better. How long have you been single?" I asked.

Just another simple question that was about to be added to my list of regrets. It's getting longer as my marathon dating journey continues. The next four hours can never be retrieved or saved. Involuntary yawning consistently happening as he tells me his woes. He has been single for only three weeks, separated from his wife and her children. Sleeping on the floor of his brother's spare room. No, it all makes sense, why he jumped at the change of a warm sofa and free meal. A quick sneaky stalk of his Facebook, as I now know his surname. Just four weeks ago, his last post was a declaration of love for the best wife in the world. Something tells me he didn't see the demise of his relationship coming. Why would he? He has the mindset of a ten-year-old still pulling pigtails of girls he likes in the playground. I feel sorrow for his wife. How did she last so long, because I would have kicked him to the kerb long ago? Three kids are enough for any woman. I want proper dates, dinners, weekends away, cosy nights in. This man is on the rebound, and my confidence has built enough to know that I deserve better than that.

The evening is ending, and to be honest, he is a nice guy, but that's it. As I walk him to the door, knowing that he is just about to be friend zoned, I fatefully decide that a kiss is in order. I have wants and needs and it has been so long since I've had a decent snog. Selfish of me to lead him on, but a kiss will confirm everything for me. Plus, a girl must get her kicks somehow and with limited options on offer, he will have to do. He doesn't know how to act, judging by the hug giving me fear my ribs are about to be broken or, at the very least, cracked. I need to release myself from the suffocating grip and what better way than to lock lips with this human? Now I have a full understanding of how to kiss bone. His lips curled inwards, his jaw grinding on my face with no tender touch. My face is full grimace under his embrace and my vagina drier that the Sahara Desert, it's time to say goodnight.

"That was nice. I will call you in the morning." I say, knowing full well my fingers will never tap his digits into my phone

Mr Rebound says...

Three weeks ago, I was happily married to the love of my life. Now here I lie on the floor of my brother's spare bedroom wondering how this has happened. I arrived home after a gig pretending to be Spiderman at a Childs birthday party. I walk into the hallway, and I spot a couple of suitcases pushed neatly into the corner. Strange? Did we have a holiday booked that somehow forgot about? Was the missus going away for work? The kids are out playing with the friends in the street, leaving the house quiet. Today was too quiet, with an eerie foreboding feeling assimilating the air. I turn the corner into the living room to find my wife perched on the edge of the couch with a stoic look on her face.

"What's up, my darling? The party was so much fun today. The look on the kids' faces when I jumped from the conservatory roof and hung upside down in the doorway was priceless."

"I've met someone else. He is moving in tomorrow. The kids like him, so you have to leave. Your brother said you can stay with him."

"I don't understand. Just yesterday you told me you loved me, we looked at holidays, we were making plans. You said you fancied Santorini, just you and me."

"I am going to Santorini. We booked it this morning, just not with you. It looks like your brother has arrived."

And just like that, my family was gone, my whole life disappeared in front of me. With no say in this decision, numb and speechless during the drive, silent in pure disbelief. Ten years we have been together, and she blindsides me this way. Who is this man who, from tomorrow, will sleep on my side of the bed, holding my wife and living with my stepchildren? While all this was happening, it hadn't even occurred to me that my brother must have known to come and pick me up so quickly.

Angry, I turn to him and ask, "How long have you known?"

"I have suspected for a while, but couldn't prove it. I didn't want to say anything in case I was wrong. While she was with him, I bumped into her at the café. She introduced him as a colleague, but they looked too friendly to be more."

"It's not your fault, bro. Just wish I had an inkling of what was going on. It doesn't feel real. Four hours ago, I was off to work, looking forward to spending the evening with her and the kids in front of the television."

"When she called and asked me to pick you up, I knew instantly what had happened. She did also say she was tired of having a child for a husband. Wanted someone with a proper job. I think it's time for you to reflect a little on your life choices. Sorry to be harsh, but she is kinda right from that aspect."

We sat the rest of the journey in silent. As we arrived at his house, he let me know I could have the spare room for as long as I needed it. Great! I'm a grown man who is now sleeping on the floor of my brother's junk room. I think I should just throw myself into dating again. Have some fun along the way.

It has only been a few hours since I left my wife and I already have profiles built on five dating apps. This is a numbers game. The more women that come across my profile, the better chance I have of being discovered. Scrolling through, I come to realise that this is not the case. The same pictures appearing as if on a constant Rolodex. The same conversation repeatedly. None of them seem like fun. I want to have a laugh and embrace my inner child, and I have had enough of adulting. If I want to dress like

Spiderman every day of my life, then that's what I am going to do. Life is too harsh, and we all need to escape. Sex, I can take it or leave it. I get everything I need from the Lycra clinging to my body. The soft fabric with a smooth touch creating friction with the hairs on my legs and chest, sending tingles to my Willie.

Chatting away to an ex-dancer online, who seems full of fun, a few mutual friends, and the love of dance in common, I ask her out on a date. She wants a daytime coffee date, which I'm happy with as being a Spidey impersonator doesn't bring in a lot of cash, I can stretch just about to treating her on this. Thankfully, it's a little nippy for spring, and the date is outside in her local park, so I can wear my bubble coat as all my other clothes are still in bin bags after the wife dropped them off. She didn't even look at me and directed all the conversation to my brother. What could I have done that was so wrong for her to treat me this way and make me feel like a pariah?

Up early and ready for date day. I can push through this. In all honesty, it's the last thing I want to do, as I'm hoping the wife will see the error of her ways and invite me back home. But in the meantime, Miss Dancer can keep me entertained. As I drive to the location, I wonder if she likes the playgrounds in parks. I think they are fun with the slides and the swings. We could do that for a while before we sit down for a drink. Dates are so formal, the interview stage to see if you meet criteria. She has already arrived; I can see her sat in her SUV waiting for me. A big cheesy smile greets me as she jumps out of the car to great me. No one has been that happy to see me in a while or has her energy levels. Chatting away on the swings, making her laugh when suddenly she stops, complains she is cold, and we should walk up to the country park for a coffee and more adult surrounding. What a buzz kill! She has just ruined the moment.

I thought she would be playful and embrace my childlike qualities. Now she wants an adult date. She rolls her eyes as I order a hot chocolate with all the trimmings. Hmmm, maybe she will not be as much fun as I thought. The country park is beautiful as she guides us down the disused canal paths. As we turn the corner, I spot another play park complete with balancing logs and sandpit. The more I get to know her, I realise what a sexual being she is. I'm not sure I could handle her. For me, being sexually intimate is messy and disgusts me. I just about manage the missionary position without disgust, and I get no actual pleasure from it. Her company is a pleasure to be around if she would only stop moaning about being cold.

Jumping up I say "Let's dance. Do the dirty dancing thing on this log."

"It's getting late and colder. Shall we just go to my house for a pizza and a movie?"

"Love that idea. I will follow you in my car."

Her house is a suburban semi-detached. When you step inside, it took you to another world. Decorated to a high standard in the latest colours. Modern but cosy. Lots of reclaimed furniture and plants with gold accents. Very tasteful, but not for me. I like natural beige colours. She offers me a drink as I settle into her big squashy sofa.

"That's mega." I said as she brings me a glass of cola decorated with dancing Santas and its own twirly straw attached. Pizza arrives, and she lets me select the movie. It's got to be a superhero movie, and there are no objections to my choice. We obviously have the same taste in movies and food. She places her head on my lap and settles in. It's a comforting feeling, as it's been a while since it happened. Cannot help wishing it was the wife, though. My entire world turned upside down and drastically changed in three weeks. She is obviously enjoying the movie as she is quiet the whole way through as we both relax in each other's company, not making a move or sound until we get to the end. A yawn escapes from her lips, obviously tired as she ushers me towards the hallway. I am unsure what to do now. Kiss Her? Hug her? What does she want? She is a dark horse and not that easy to read, so I go for one of my friend hugs, nice and tight. The wife said they made her feel safe.

Her dark eyes are looking up at me, requesting a kiss. Not sure how to go about this, as I'm not good with saliva, I tighten my lips and go for the kill. At first, she seems to enjoy it but becomes less responsive as we carry on. She smiles warmly at me as she walks me to the door.

"That was nice. I will call you in the morning."

She never calls. Not arsed

Mr Copy and paste

A girl's night is on the cards and it's my turn to host. Everything is prepared. Vodka, gin, wine, and Jaeger bombs. A plethora of snacks on demand. I've missed the girls so much with my attention taken away by my many misdemeanours with the opposite sex. The music is blasting; the drinks are flowing; the chatter is getting louder. Out of the speaker, we hear Wham rap. Transported back to our teenage years, jumping onto the sofa and the coffee table, singing with the full capacity of our lungs, then a smooth transition into Duran Duran, Girls on film. How I have missed this, the camaraderie while prancing and twerking in my latest onesie. Behind me, I hear the collapse of the familiar sound of the cracking of the coffee table.

Turning round just in time to see my best friend fall to the ground on her back, with her legs in the air, showing the room the full delights of her tummy control pant. Squeals of uncontrollable laughter as we pile on top of each other, just the same way we did in high school whenever one of the group fell.

The sisterhood remains as strong now as it did back then.

Need to bring this down a notch or two before my complete house ends up cracked and splintered. I leap onto the TV cabinet while banging a spoon against my glass.

"Attention! Attention ladies! I have got a brilliant idea. Let's play a game. Five beautiful ladies, all unlucky in love, so it's time to have fun with it. Let me introduce you to the world of Tinder bingo!"

Raucous cheers and eyes full of mischief as we run for our phones. Fresh bottles of wine and a delightful serving of nachos in the centre of the table were ready to go. The first one to match and engage with a brunette, blonde, ginger, a small one and a tall one wins, and the next night out is free. If we all match the same guy and converse, we treat ourselves to a weekend spa trip in a fancy hotel.

"Ten minutes ladies, work your magic and get swiping!"

I always win, swiping every profile with no idea of what they look like. My friends, still tindering the old school way. Checking out what the guys have to say, wondering if they would fancy them in the real world. In this competition, that is the only way to lose. The fools all seem to have forgotten how competitive I am and what a horrible loser I am. I even cheat when playing monopoly with the kids.

The phones ping relentlessly. It's busy tonight in Tinder world. I have matched with all the guys on the list, now I just need to get them to talk.

"Bingo, I win. The drinks are on you lot." I announce maybe too eagerly. Groans and mutters around the table. A high five from the bestie with a little too much force. The rest of the girls grabbing my phone to validate the result.

The girls laugh manically, when one exclaims, "You realise we have all matched on the same guy? How about we all message him at the same time and see what the response is?"

The same look of knowing mischief is about to occur flashed across our faces simultaneously. An excitable discussion for the opening line creating an electrifying union between us all. When we are together and alcohol is involved, it becomes more difficult to restrain our behaviour, each egging the other on. The poor man is about to unknowingly enter the lair of the wolf and be brutalised. I almost feel sorry for him and with another swig of vodka that soon dissipates. The opener agreed upon, keeping it simple and friendly.

"Hey handsome, it's good to match." SEND!

I very much doubt that he is going to respond to all of us. We are so different from each other that we sometimes question how we are all such good friends. The vibration of the phones on the table with an orchestral sound of notifications coming one after another. It's too late to turn back and put a stop to this unacceptable behaviour, as we concur to read the message out at the same time.

"Hi there, you have got to be the most beautiful woman I have seen on Tinder. I feel lucky you picked me to match with.", five voices say in unison.

Fuck me, he has replied with the same message to us all. We all concur that we must get him into sex talk as quickly as possible. Bestie number one is the best at this. She loves nothing more than being sat on the sofa in her pyjamas, a glass of cold Chablis and sexy talk to get her in the mood for her nightly masturbation ritual. I'm surprised she has a clitoris left from the battering it takes with her supercharged plug-in vibrators. She often comes up with the excuse that it is environmentally friendly, plus the factor of frustration with the sheer volume of batteries she was buying. We just think her magic button has gone numb and needs the extra power.

A different text sent by each of us, all eluding to sexual intent. This guy must think he is sexier than sliced bread. Five older horny women all wanting him to do unspeakable things to them. The manipulation of a man came easily with the blatant wanting of the messages. One benefit of being older is that you are no longer concerned with the thought's others may have of you. No worries about the judgements of your behaviour and actions. A flurry of texts messages exchanged between one man versus five women. You got the sense that the poor delusional creature on the other side of this menopausal bombardment thought he was the dog's bollocks. A super stud. He certainly wasn't the most attractive man I had ever seen, or the most intelligent one I had conversed with. He possessed an off the scale level of arrogance that just made him more fun to toy with, like a cat playing with its prey before it goes in for the kill.

No matter the message of any of us, we all received the same reply. His skill at copy and paste on a mobile device was supreme. How many others was he talking to, I wonder, and how many of them were wearing their own wine goggles? I also wonder if any other pack of females plays Tinder bingo.

"You are the only one that I'm excited about. I have stopped talking to all my other matches. None of them have held my interest," he states boldly to us all, as we have reached a junction for the next step. A mutual democratic decision, with a clink of glasses to confirm our unity at this team sport. We all text him our WhatsApp numbers. We leave him for a while, so he has time to enter our contact details into his phone, and five minutes later, there it is. The first dick pic of the night. Now we are really getting somewhere.

"Tell me your favourite sexual fantasy. Mine is to have a threesome with a hot guy and a blonde woman."

"Have you ever thought about having a threesome?"

"What are your thoughts are group sex?"

"Have you ever been to a sex club?"

"Do you like to share? I have always wanted to have sex with a woman and a man together. Do you know anyone who we could ask to be involved? Not on the first time we meet up, obviously. That would be just about you and me!"

Five leading messages sent. Will he take the bait and jump straight in? The phones vibrate in unison.

"I have had plenty of threesomes," he brags, "I know four other women that have asked for group sex. I could arrange it if you were willing?"

Quick preparation as we each take a selfie, gain approval from the group, and send.

"Oh my! That is a delicious thought. What if I don't fancy them? She would have to have big boobs. Do you have any pictures of them?"

One by one we all sent a similar message, full of promise of the salacious time on offer. His reply was swift, with pictures of my gang delivered to my phone, with a simple reply, "They have all said they are up for it. We should get this arranged. I had a feeling you were my perfect woman when I swiped on you. This is fate!"

"Thats so sweet of you to say," I replied. "Let me know where and when."

The conversation carried on for another thirty minutes, give or take a few, before we were all tired of the mundane shit he was talking about. Sexting with someone you don't find remotely appealing or have any sexual intention towards becomes boring. One group selfie later and we are ready to come out into the open and admit our ruse. Ready, steady, go. Five accounts, same picture, all sent. There is always one girl in the group that feels bad and regrets her actions when sozzled.

"Do you think we are being mean?"

"One hundred per cent." We all shout back at her, again bringing us too an uncontrollable laughter, while the bestie falls off her chair, trying to contain her snorts.

"You absolute bunch of bitches. I will make sure you never go out in this city again. No one will want you by the time I have finished. See You Next Tuesday!" Guess he is not happy about how the events of the evening have transpired as I grab another bottle of prosecco from the fridge, still perplexed that he can't even use a proper swear word.

"Beyonce anyone?"

All the single ladies emanating from the speaker as we all try to pull off the dance routine to the best of our drunken ability.

Mr Copy and paste says...

I have little luck with the ladies. They all think I'm strange. I get nervous around them and act like a complete dick. It can't be helped; I get the scent of a woman, and something happens to me. Online dating seems to be the best arena for me. It's easy to portray a confident, successful guy. The men I have a round me have no such issues. While they are members of the golf club, I work there. They have money and fast cars, whereas I park the cars and wait for them to give me money as a tip. This presents me with many opportunities to grab a photo with the cars and the caddies and pass them off as my own in my profile.

The pretence this allows me in my imaginary world brings forth the type of guy all the women want. If a date comes out of it, I can usually arrange them for when the club is busy. I borrow one car and arrive. Straight away they are usually impressed with the array of vehicles I turn up in and I use the "I have to get back to the club" line as I have probably told them my family owns it and there is an urgent matter that needs tending to. I can tell tales I have picked up from listening to the discussions overheard in the bar and manipulate until they become second nature to me, and I believe my own bullshit. By doing this, I become the man I want to be.

The best policy is to swipe every profile I come across until I have run out. The odds in my favour. There must be someone in the virtual world that will see my profile and want to match with me. Not being the most confident bloke, I have a list of lines in my notes that I can just copy and paste my responses. How will they ever know? It's not likely they would ever know each other.

Tonight is a successful swiping mission. I've matched with five older ladies in less than a minute, all of them messaging me almost instantly. Thank the lord that I have all my replies pre-prepared. These women all want me, all of them have turned the conversation to sex and if I play my cards right, I could get my leg over for the whole of next week. Usually, I wouldn't go for ladies old enough to be my mum, or even my grandma, if they had their babies young enough.

Of course, I tell them they are all beautiful, even if I feel as though I am scraping the barrel. I'm not into older women, but my thoughts are that they are more likely to be grateful for whatever they can get. Plus, from listening to some of the locker room talk, the older they are, the naughtier they get. There has got to be at least one of these pensioners who will allow me to explore some kinky activities. I have always wondered if it was in me, and if so, what would my kinks be? I often wonder what it feels like to be tied up, spanked with a leather paddle, or even whipped. One thing for sure is that I wouldn't want a woman stamping on my balls in her favourite heels. I've been kicked in that region a few times, hurt like hell, and have very little understanding of the joy of such an activity.

Now the conversation has moved to WhatsApp. The copy and paste becomes easier. Not even necessary to put the hard work in, it's just a case of writing the message to one of them and then forwarding the message to the rest. All of them want threesomes and group sex, a meeting I am happy to arrange. After asking them all for photos of themselves, only to proceed sending them onto the other women engaging with. The frisson of excitement building within me. The anticipation of fulfilling a lifelong wish about to become true. I need to impress the boys with my stories. Sign of a real man that can handle five women at once and keep his pecker going long enough to ensure satisfaction for them all.

I could not have planned this any better if I tried. The descriptions of the females they would willingly have sex with magically match the others. If I wasn't in the moment and it wasn't happening to me, I never would have believed this was all real. Usually this is the type of locker room banter I hear, whilst being invisible to the narrators. I am finally going to be accepted into the popular clique at the club. No longer just the caddy, I will be one of them. Raising the bar on their exploits. They will beg me to join enter their fold. There is only one girl I am not warming to. She seems to be full of herself, also coming across drunk and underlying bitchy tendencies. She is the one I want to choke during sex and get her to call me Daddy, put her in her place and let her know who she is dealing with.

One by one, they all return my messages, stating they find each other attractive, even beautiful. The bitchy one complained they weren't her usual type, but she was happy to lower her standards if it meant she could enjoy the experience with me. She had better like it rough, as she is getting what she deserves. Never have I felt so turned on by the dislike of another person before, but she has a magnificent set of breasts on her. Now that I have the agreement with them all, I let them all know that I will be busy planning the activities this week and l will let them know. Best tip I have ever overheard, this copy and paste stuff. Just tell them what they want to hear, and you get everything you want. Women are so stupid and easy to fool.

The last messages of the night from my harem appeared on my screen. How on earth has this happened? They all know each other, all chummy and best of friends. They have been tricking me all this time. If I didn't have the evidence in front of me, I would never believe that this could happen to me. Immediately transported back to high school, the torment placed on me by the mean girls, with rich daddies and athletic boyfriends. It's happening all over again in adulthood. These women have mocked and bullied me, purely for their entertainment.

"You absolute bunch of bitches. I will make sure you never go out in this city again. No one will want you by the time I have finished! See You Next Tuesday!" They will be sorry they ever crossed me!

.

Mr Alpine Pop Man

Who the hell is the Alpine pop man? Full of childhood memories growing up in a working-class family of Liverpool, during the seventies. Pop or soda was a luxury. Today, it's in every shop with millions of varieties. We had orangeade, dandelion and burdock, cola, and lemonade. Even then, it was a treat on the rare occasions you went out for a meal. Times were tough, with an energy crisis, power cuts, three day working weeks and forced to wear brown flared corduroy jeans and velour sweaters by your parents.

This era held a certain amount of freedom for children. We were not yet aware of the term political correctness, and everybody spoke their mind, regardless of the brutality their words contained. Myself and my friends played in the streets until our mothers screeched our names for dinner. For miles we would explore, climbing trees, investigating abandoned houses, entering places that our parents would cast as off limits. If they ever found us, the adventure of our days was more important than the punishment we would face. The one thing that would bring us all running home bells of the Alpine pop man arriving in his yellow truck with bottles rattling filled with a kaleidoscope of colours and fizz.

The alpine pop man was a local hero in a six-year-old eyes. He brought promise and adventure, plus money as we went around doors to steal the bottles left out to gain the two pence return money. His instantly recognisable in his yellow and yellow jacket. Kids hanging off the side of the truck, waiting to pinch a couple of bottles while the driver's back was turned. No regard for the risk of their lives. Getting a free bottle of sarsaparilla, pineappleade or American cream soda gave you kudos from the gang of latch key kids roaming the streets. To this day I can see a can of Dandelion and Burdock on the shelves of a shop and the memories of a free childhood fill my memories with smiles.

A new match has come through, my opening line typed

"What was your favourite flavour from the Alpine pop man?"

"My dad was an Alpine pop man! Always has plenty of tropical fruit flavour in the house. What was your flavour?"

"Ha-ha. No way! I would have loved my dad to have that job, instead of convincing himself he was a professional gambler and would have a big win one day. My flavour was Pineapple"

For weeks we spoke before we met. He said he was a sapiosexual and liked to get to know people on an intellectual level before going out on a date. Wasn't too sure what that was, but went with it anyway. He didn't ask if I understood what it meant either, presuming I knew. Now that we had common ground, after weeks of chatting, I was getting bored. We needed to meet. It was now or never, as I don't want a pen pal. The more I pushed, the more he stepped back. What was he waiting for? He always initiated the conversation, showing he must be interested in me.

"I've got a surprise for you. I'm going to send you a picture. It's not a dick pic. I think you will like it."

From previous experience, when they say it's not a dick pic, it usually is but restyled. Do I even want to look? Oh, fuck it! By this point, I've seen so many. What harm is one more going to do? I need to open the message several times, blinking hard to refresh my eyes. Was it my imagination, or did I just see him completely naked apart from an Alpine jacket?

"When are we going for dinner?"
I'm not too sure what he is inviting me to eat, but at least he has proven he has got a pair of balls and

used them to finally request a date. Revealing he has been holding off until the jacket arrived from eBay. Good for him, making all that effort, scouring online auctions to impress me and appeal to my deranged form of humour. Tomorrow night I will arrive in all my finery, perfect makeup. Money spent on a professional manicure and trip to the hair salon. I need to impress him, as my gut is telling me to have a good feeling about this one. Why do I have to be eternally optimistic? It's so annoying.

A nice simple bistro is the setting for tonight's date. Nothing to over the top, music at the right level so you can hear the conversation held at the table for two with dimmed lighting and candle in the centre of the table. A setting made for romance. A place to fall in love. Hands held across the table with locked eyes, seeing deep inside. A wave of emotion as hope reignites. Could it be true, Mr Right is sitting opposite me? Have I come to the end of my quest to find love with all the trials, tribulations, and tests put before me throughout my journey? Nothing will impede my happiness sat before me. I just have to make sure my mood swings stay in check, as they can seriously do some damage. The hormones flying up and down, leading to irrational decisions. Most of the time I can never remember the names of my own children, now I will have to remember his. Let's hope the average-looking man before me for whom I am prepared to settle for does nothing to irritate me.

"I loved the photo you sent me. It was so fucking funny. Totally unexpected." I said with through a teasing smile. "Are you going to wear it in the bedroom for me?"

His response was sharp and unexpected.

"You will never receive another one. I find sending naked pictures beneath me, and so should you. Also, do not swear again. I told you I am a sapiosexual, and it is your intelligence that attracts me. No partner of mine will speak in that manner"

Do I rise above this, let it go and move on? My willingness to give him another chance surprised me. His efforts at dominance, strangely turning me on, imaging the onset of a sexual relationship filled with role play. Ready to explore all varieties of sexual activities with this man. I will open myself to be submissive for his sexual thrills, wanting to share his Sapio thrills with him. Still don't know what this entails, but it sounds kinky.

The evening draws to a close as he escorts me to a taxicab with a simple, gentle kiss to bid me goodnight. He is a gentleman; it seems. Not the usual approach I encounter on Tinder. Men on dating apps, keen to promote their testosterone levels, and fulfil their bachelor dreams by spreading their sperm deposits across the city. The pleasant change to be treated as a lady and not a free prostitute was a welcome relief.

For six weeks, we met twice a week. Always at the same restaurant, at the same time and days. A routine that at first felt safe was now becoming dull. I am all for taking things slow and getting to know each other better, but I need to discover the sexual freedom menopause brings. The knowledge that not having periods any longer allows a revolution within oneself. The dismissal of panic attacks when you are a few days late signalling the fear of pregnancy. But I need to copulate while I still have oestrogen in my body and a libido that still allows desire.

If he doesn't make a move tonight, make me feel desired, then a new profile will have to be built. He needs to understand that. To keep my attention alive and directed at him, he will have to come up with the goods and he will have to move fast before I go on holiday next month. With no fulfilment, a wandering eye will develop. Tonight, the conversation was the same usual bullshit. Polite and engaging.

"What books have you read this week? He asked while still with his eyes concentrated on the pasta dinner before him. The carbonara here is divine, but would it be too much to ask for him to at least look at me when he asks a question.

"What are we?" I respond.

"I've never heard of that. Is it a philosophical textbook? Biology maybe?"

"No, it's a simple question. What are we? Are we friends, partners or casual acquaintances that meet to eat dinner and discuss the meaning of life? Are we ever going to take this to the next level?"

"Do you want to move it forward?"

"I wouldn't be asking if I didn't. I don't understand why you don't"

"I do. I needed to make sure you were ready. After dinner, would you like to stay the night at my house?"

A quick check in my bag, making sure that my toothbrush and fresh panties are still there. I have carried them to every date with him, refusing to give up. He is stable, has a good job and will surely be an agreeable companion, which is what I need in life. I need to forgo the excitement, danger and all the physical attraction. Need to let it go and settle for someone who will be good for me. The doubts creep in as we drive to his house in silence. I am in unfamiliar territory; in a part of town, I have never visited. The houses are showing an area with obvious wealth in a gated community.

We talk in depth about lots of intellectual things, but now as I enter his home, it becomes apparent I know nothing about him. The house is a shrine to his dead wife. I didn't even know he was a widow. Each picture of her surrounded by candles and religious artifacts. He guides me through his home straight to the bedroom. This is not a room he uses; the wardrobes are empty with an absence of trinkets on the dressing table and a perfectly made bed that has never seen a crumpled bedsheet from the passionate lovemaking. Too many questions that I should have asked before I struggling to leave my mouth.

Left alone in that room with only a small illumination of the moon through the vertical blinds, waiting in silence for him to return with wine, a brilliant idea springs to mind. Let's liven this party up a little. Of course, I'm a genius! Lightbulb moment! He needs me to bring the spice to the occasion. The quiet sound of his feet climbing the stairs. By the time he enters the room, I will be ready for him. My dress lies in a heap on the floor, as I lay naked apart from stiletto heels and his tie around my neck. The light of the moon catching my curves as I wait for my new lover to enter. I hear his pause with a sharp inhale as he stands in the doorway, allowing his eyes to feast on my body.

Throwing a white flannel nightgown in my direction, I could smell the scent of stale perfume. "Cover yourself, then lay still on your back."
This was not a request, but an order. I am so confused that I go along with it all for a moment. They plunged the room into darkness as he shuts out the last slither of light through the blinds. The cool touch of his breath as climbs on top of me., lifting the nightgown to my waist. He is naked from the waist down as his hardness pushes against my thighs. Are my ears deceiving me?
"Who the fuck is Elizabeth? Why are you calling me that name? It's not my name! Get the fuck off me!"
His face contorted with screaming anger. "Don't you ever say her name! How dare you put her name in the same sentence as a swear word. You are not worthy enough to say her name"
"I am only going to ask you one more time, before I lose my shit on you! Who the fuck is Elizabeth?"

"My wife, you are wearing her nightgown, standing in her house. You should be grateful. Not one woman has been here since she died ten years ago. But now, I realise this is a huge mistake and you are nothing but a whore! Get out of my house!"

Thankful to the whizz kid who came up with Uber, who once again was coming to my rescue.

Mr Alpine pop man says...

Ten years ago, my beautiful Elizabeth died. My world has never been the same since. No one could compare to her beauty, both inside and out. Her levels of intelligence and her moral beliefs were all I could ask for in a wife. What she ever saw in me, I will never know. Loneliness for a companion has led me to try online dating. From the very beginning, I make it clear that I am a Sapiosexual. It is intelligence that attracts me, and the ability to hold a conversation would be a pleasant change. Recent dates have left me with no desire to continue for a second one.

My list of requirements for a future partner is simple. Long dark hair, slim build, ladylike behaviour, and being able to accompany me to church on Sundays. My religion is as important to me as it was to my wife. We made our best memories through the community of mass and gospels. No children came out of our marriage, no matter how hard we tried. Elizabeth would have loved to have at least a son, but it was never to be. She would have been a wonderful mother. I know this to be true. How could she not be? Even though she didn't bear me children, she was still perfect. There is surely no harm in going on a few dates, but that is where it is going to end for me. Sex is not a top priority for me, having only ever performed the missionary position. If you can't go forth and create, then what is the point? I get no enjoyment from it whatsoever. Not too sure why I have matched with this one. She looks a little frivolous, very sexual, and not my type at all. There is a look of Elizabeth about her, though, her doppelgänger.

"What was your favourite flavour from the Alpine pop man?"

Interesting opening, showing her intelligence to create a conversation starter. A question loaded with information about herself and knowing the answer would give her knowledge without having to deal with twenty minutes of dull small talk. I am very impressed with the cleverness of it all. Not only does she get you to think of something that is warm and familiar, but straight away she knows your age, background, and your social class.

"My dad was an Alpine pop man. Always plenty of tropical fruit in our house. What was your flavour?"

"Ha-ha. No way! I would have loved my dad to have that job, instead of convincing himself he was a professional gambler and would have a big win one day. My flavour was Pineapple"

I found myself drawn to this woman. She has a good sense of morality, could hold a conversation, and was well read. It is so refreshing to meet a working-class woman with aspirations to improve herself and become socially mobile. Not allowing her background to hold her back from her ambitions in life. For weeks we spoke, by text, phone and even video calling, bringing out of my comfort zone into a false sense of security. At night, I would go to bed and imagine making love to her, her face melding into that of my wife's. They have brought her to me through the power of prayer. The enticement of her bringing me wanting her to the forefront of my mind. The carnal lust was playing with my head, the thoughts that convinced me there was a higher force at play.

Every Sunday, I confessed the sins of my thoughts after mass, and still went home with depraved wishes of her. This weekend, everything changed when I took steps to enter her world. A parcel waiting for me on the doorstep. Could I do this? Would I be able to repent for the sin I was about to commit? Peeling back the paper to reveal a childhood memory of my father. His voice as he came through the front door after a long day on the truck in his bright green and yellow jacket, armed with a plethora of flavours from Alpine pop. Laughter and joy this man brought to our lives to be cruelly taken by cancer on my tenth birthday impacted all the decisions I have made to this day. Seeking refuge within the church to find the answers. The day I raised from prayer and my knees to find Elizabeth smiling back at me, with a halo of light surrounding her, my being became whole as all I asked for was answered within those walls. One year later, we married in that same church.

Please forgive me for what I am about to do. Naked beneath the jacket, I sent a picture with the tag line "Would you like to go for dinner?" The response was instantaneous. The bistro I have invited her to join me for dinner is the same one I brought my wife. We dined here twice a week in the beautiful romantic surrounding, eating the same meal and drinking the same wine, discussing the latest current affairs, books we had read. My hope for this lady was that she could keep up the high standards already set. I will not drop my standards, as I am already annoyed that I have let myself down. Deep in the knowledge of my faith was being tested with temptation.

For weeks we met twice a week, same table. I ate my usual order while she changed hers every time, wanting to sample everything on the menu; the waiters coveting her, jumping to her every command. Her face was full of questions this evening. There was something different about her energy, a nervousness that she had not displayed before. There is a coldness between us that has developed over the course of the evening. I need to change the atmosphere.

"What books have you read this week?" I ask without looking up from my spaghetti arrabiatta.

"What are we?" I respond.

"I've never heard of that. Is it a philosophical textbook? Biology maybe?"

"No, it's a simple question. What are we? Are we friends, partners or casual acquaintances that meet to eat dinner and discuss the meaning of life? Are we ever going to take this to the next level?"

"Do you want to move it forward?"

"I wouldn't be asking if I didn't. I don't understand why you don't"

"I do. I needed to make sure you were ready. After dinner, would you like to stay the night at my house?"

Silence in the taxi home, as she stares in wonder at the magnificent mansions surrounding us. It obviously impressed her, placing a doubt in my mind that she is materialistic, and wants to be with me for how I can provide for her. My wife never worked. I was happy to provide for both of us, even if she couldn't provide me with children. The house is in darkness, only the moonlight coming in through the blinds dispersing some shadows, catching the metal of the crucifixes hung on the walls framing pictures of my beautiful wife. Her eyes swiftly glance over at them as I guide her to the spare bedroom. I could never be unfaithful to Elizabeth by letting this woman sleep in her bed. The room is devoid of any personal items, memories, or belongings. I leave her to gather herself without turning on the light. A quick look back to see how the light of the night catches her face. My heart plunges as I see Elizabeth's features over hers. Is it a blessing or a warning? Why has she come back to me now? Did she just need a vessel to speak to me, allow me to make love to her again one last time?

Downstairs, I open a closet containing Elizabeth's belongings. The smell of her floral perfume filling my senses as I retrieve one of her nightgowns.

Another sign that she is upstairs waiting for me to reignite our union. She has always been here, never left, her soul watching over me and now I have delivered to her the body she needs to return. I can hear her moving onto the bed with the creak of the springs to lie in wait for me. My breaths become deeper as I watch her beautiful curves under the moon. Creeping towards her, I pass her the gown. We have never made love naked, so I am surprised at her boldness. Closing the blinds to shut out the last sliver of light, the room plunges into darkness, while I raise her gown to her waist and push my hardness into her.

"How I have missed you, Elizabeth. You have come back to me. Something will never separate again us.

"Who the fuck is Elizabeth? Why are you calling me that name? It's not my name! Get the fuck off me!"

Feeling how contorted my face had become screaming with anger, "Don't you ever say her name! How dare you put her name in the same sentence as a swear word. You are not worthy to say her name."

"I am only going to ask you one more time, before I lose my shit on you! Who the fuck is Elizabeth?"

"My wife, you are wearing her nightgown, standing in her house. You should be grateful. Not one woman has been here since she died ten years ago. But now, I realise this is a huge mistake and you are nothing but a whore! Get out of my house!"

I hear the Uber pull up outside the house while I sit on the edge of the bed, tears falling from my eyes, hanging my head in shame. I have fallen under the spell of a witch who came to test my faith. How will Elizabeth ever be able to forgive me?

Mr Way Too Young

I have never been more excited about getting to the airport. Still traumatised that the last man to enter my life thought I was his dead wife. How could it possibly get any worse? I am done! No more online dating for me! I do not want to hear no more about it. I have bought another cat, the beautiful beast that he is. His face allows me to wake for with a smile every morning. He wants nothing from me apart from cuddles and food, happy to keep me warm at night with no complaints and consoles me when I feel blue.

The taxi pulls up to the departures terminal with the bestie waving insanely, holding a bottle of vodka in hand. It's six am, no better time to get pissed than at the gates of freedom and adventure. We need this to try our feeble attempts at flirting through security, knowing we had packed too many liquids and too tight to pay for hold luggage. I sail through with my best smile, while the bestie gets almost up to a strip search. Every fucking time! We can't go anywhere without her getting the attention of the authorities. In her head, it's because she is so hot that they need the excuse to talk to her, but in mine it's because she is so noticeable. Long blonde curly hair, petite in stature but with a foghorn voice full of northern bravado. You would think she has just stepped off the longships in Lindisfarne Viking invasions, ready to contest the thrones and conquer the lands with its men.

The flight to Dublin keeps you in the air for twenty-five minutes, before you land on the beautiful Celtic lands of Ireland. The weather gods are with us as the sun is cracking the flags. Straight off to hire a completely inappropriate convertible car to experience our Thelma and Louise's menopausal moments with handbags stuffed with incontinence pads, cigarettes, and phone's camera ready to guide us to our destination that we have forgotten to charge. It can't be that hard to find the west Atlantic coast and the pretty town of Galway. Leaving Dublin behind to visit last on our road trip. The orienteering skills we picked up as kids when all that was available were your local maps picked up on petrol stations, ready to put to the test. Would be a good start if we knew which way up the map was supposed to be.

Two hours and several toll roads later, we arrive in the pretty picturesque town of Clare Galway.

Beautiful hotel, in stunning surroundings, but miles away from the coast. Our neighbours, the ruins of the friary and castle. I am fascinated with the medieval and Tudor times; you cannot visit Ireland without falling into a trip back in time of battlefields and the rich history of the invasions of armies of Henry VIII. It would have been nicer if the company available were not Francian monks buried in the graveyard. After an hour of touring the abbey, the need for conversation with men who had a pulse was pulling, so off to the city to see the sights. Galway, the city of the Claddagh Museum, allowing us to buy rings hoping it might change our luck with the opposite sex and let all the Irish beauties we could meet, signalling to them we are single and available to be approached. I am willing to believe in anything. I'll move to my ancestral home if I must.

A dinner of fresh oysters and Guinness, tired from the sea air, we make our way back to the hotel. A wedding is taking place in the ballroom, it would be rude not to crash it. Quick shower and a smarten up, we enter the room to the dulcet deep tone of Polish voices. Traditional music playing with lots of backslapping and tales of home being told. In all honesty, they could have been telling dirty jokes, but whatever they were saying sounded interested and funny. As hard as we tried to stay inconspicuous, the drinks were free and the shackles of being the uninvited guests becoming loose. The sensation of being pulled towards a handsome young man was strong. Fighting with the impulse to talk to this man that was at least twenty years my junior was a struggle. Fresh air and a cigarette beckoned, even though I had packed in the dirty habit five years ago. Blaming on the vodka and lime, as I always do, I made my way to the smoking area behind the hotel. A wind was picking up, encouraging goosebumps on the skin. Thankful for the patio heaters and the soft cushioned bench, anger at my stupidity of caving to the cravings of nicotine, the unlit cigarette hanging from my lips while I ponder on whether to spark it up or throw it to the ground.

The flame feels warm on my face, looking up to see the owner of the lighter. Smiling back at me, the gorgeous creature I had spotted earlier in the ballroom. Had he followed me out here? That's an interesting turn of events! I can't help but to smile back, inviting him to sit next to me.

"Are you English?" His Polish accent was thick with a sexy Irish lilt.

"Yes, I am here for a holiday. Not sure on where to go and what to see. Any ideas?"

"I can show you around if you would like that. I have been in Ireland for two years. I know my way round."

Who was this man before me? The pull towards him was insane. It had been a long time since I had met someone in the flesh to whom I had an instant attraction to. The flirting between us felt natural, his energy youthful and exuberant, matching my own. He abandoned his friends to join me and the bestie in the bar, willing to spend his crypto on our drinks. Aiming to impress. First thoughts of a harmless flirtation being to pass as I rested my hand on his knee, pulling myself closer to him; feel the warmth of his body next to mine. The communication was easy between us, laughing at the same jokes with a matching brutality and sharpness.

"Let me take you home, give you a massage and good sex!" before kissing me with such passion and fervour. My body responding to his advances, the pain in my groin with pure wanting, that if we hadn't had been in a public place, for definite we would have sealed the deal, right there and then. My legs wrapped around his waist while sitting on a bench, with no care for who could observe us. Carefree and oblivious to the world, inside an internal struggle was happening. He was only thirty years old. I needed to stop this before I fuck him up with my distended view on the world. On the other hand, I would never see him again, as I would be back home in another country in four days.

Every time I tried to stop and pull away from him, he pulled me closer and tighter. "Why are you trying to escape me? You are mine now!"

"I am too old for you by at least twenty years. You are coming to the age when you want to settle down. I'm fifty. Why on earth would you be interested in an old woman?"

Sliding back on the bench, looking at me with fierce intensity and shock. He had a way of looking into my soul, with a deep knowledge of me, even though it had only been a few hours.

"I thought you were only a couple of years older than me. It doesn't bother me. I am comparing you to other women that I have met tonight, and I realise they are just girls. As soon as I saw you, I knew you were the one that I want!"

There is something special about this man, familiar to me even though we had only just come across each other. He felt like home. He was goddam sexy, and that was a bonus. The snogging continued in the back seat of the taxi, with a break for a stop of at the twenty-four-hour store to purchase condoms, destiny sealed with the exchange of the Euros to the attendant. The rest of the drive, lips locked together, only coming up for air as we arrived at his home. A semi-detached in an up-and-coming area of Knocknacarra, miles away from the safety net of my hotel and abandoned bestie.

Standing in the warm night air, a sudden search for keys to enter, to no avail. We are locked out. How the hell are we going to get in? A knowing look at each other, then upwards to the open window and drainpipes. The same idea in both our heads. We are going to have to scale the walls and climb in. Nothing new to me and him, it seems. The number of times I had to do this when younger and missing my curfew gave me plenty of practice. A rehearsal leading up to this moment of urgency. The sooner I ripped this man's clothes from his body, the better. A holiday fling was exactly what I needed. After my last disaster, I was determined not to get attached.

First up the pipe, as he pushed me up, getting a grope of my bottom at the same time. His hands too close to my nether regions, making my clit pulse, swelling in my pants. Reaching for the window, I fall in, landing on his bed. Quick scan of the room alerts me to the fact that he was not expecting anyone to come over tonight. Clothes, ashtrays and general junk scattered everywhere with unmade sheets. Don't ask me why, but the mess comforted me. I lean out of the window to grab his hand and pull him the last way, though, landing on top of me, straight into a kiss and the ripping off clothes from each other. The buttons on his shirt flying across the room with ferocious intent.

His hand crawls inside me, giving me pleasure I had not felt for many years. Within two minutes, the release of an orgasm came, followed by the waterfall of ejaculation, lowering his lips to my pussy to drink my juices. There was no way to hold back the next waves of pleasure that followed. The dam gates had been opened. To be honest, I might have just pissed myself, hard to tell the difference these days! Regardless of whatever fluid was leaving my urethra, it felt insane, and I needed more from him "Pieprz mnie!"

For a moment he stopped, looking at me, stunned.

"You speak Polish?"

"At little, but only the most important words. Not sure of the correct masculine and feminine words. So, as I said before, Fuck me, Proszę!"

"Z przyjemnością"

"The pleasure is all mine. Now come here and stop talking."

He did not need asking twice, his cock rigid as it plunged inside of me, creating a groan of pleasure from us both. He fit me perfectly. His had body ramming against me with the vigour and intensity you would expect of a young man, our eyes not letting go of each other. A film of sweat glistening across our bodies, reaching climax together. His skin feeling clammy as he collapses on top of me clutching his chest. His face contorted with pain, rolling onto the bed.

"I can't breathe. My heart hurts."

The heat generating from his body, with a feverish break out as his own system fights the temperature. Fuck me, he is having a heart attack. What do I do? Standing naked in his room, on top of his rubble, unsure of the next steps to take. Uncaring of my nudity, rushing to the bathroom to get a cold wet towel to cool him down, slamming straight into his housemate, who was unaware of my presence in his home.

"I think I've killed him. He's having a heart attack. Help me!"

Perplexed, he stood rooted to the spot. Confused at the naked woman standing in front of him, unsure of why she claims his young friend was on the brink of death.

"Are you on drugs?"

"Seriously, why would you ask that? I need help, not sarcasm!"

Trying my best to cool down my handsome young thing, swearing under my breath. Why does this shit always happen to me? He's, not even old or rich. What is the benefit to me? Raspy breath with quiet words uttering from his lips.

"I think I have taken too much cocaine."

"Are you fucking kidding me? How did you get a hard on?" as I spot a half smoked spliff laying in the ashtray. The same of weed makes me feel queasy, but it's either that or leave him lying there with his heart racing from the aftereffect of indulging in the class A or let him get stoned. The latter option seems to be the perfect solution. Should I join him and get on his wavelength? The room was filling with the sweet saccharin scent of skunk with cloudy plumes of smoke. It worked, much to my relief, with my own heartbeat coming back to normal. Full of apologies and embarrassment, he holds me close to him as I fall asleep with my head on his chest, listening to the rhythm of his heart falling into place with mine.

The next morning spent with a slower pace of lovemaking, brought closer together with the madness of the night before. I wasn't prepared to leave him just yet, to go back to a life of emptiness. At this present moment, I could feel love for this man, who was totally unsuitable for me, miles away from home. The cocoon we placed ourselves in for the next four days held a fear of being broken. I moved him into the hotel with us, guilt at leaving my bestie to her own devices. The days spent together, the three of us as we drove up the West Atlantic coast road, stopping to sunbathe on the golden sand beaches of Silver Strand, with is clear blue water and restaurants with an incredible array of seafood on offer. The nights spent enjoying each other's bodies with an astonishing display of stamina.

Today is the day to leave for Dublin. The sadness felt inside me, wishful that I could throw my life away and stay here by his side. The parting hug was the hardest, with a kiss full of our need for each other.

"We will see each other again. The angels have brought you to me. This is meant to be. Zegnaj na razie piękna."

One last kiss before I climb in the car, "Do widzenia" The hardest goodbye I have ever said. My heart broken with the impending doom of separation and panic of never falling asleep or waking up with him again. Watching him, watching me as I drive away in the rear-view mirror.

Unable to enjoy the thrills of Dublin, walking spent of energy, still feeling him between my legs from this morning's athletic marathon of sex. Memories of him bringing the occasional smile to my face. I was already pining for him. The bestie doing her best to cheer me up with little success. Numb inside as I sat on the plane ready to take me off this island, further away from someone I had fallen in love with so quickly. He would forget me as soon as the next girl stepped into his view. My insecurities creeping into my whole being. A bright young thing with her whole life ahead of her, or me with my menopausal madness and baggage of experiences. The phone turned off to resist the temptation of staring at his photos and messages.

Landing on the tarmac of my city airport, knowing I would have to reconnect with the world by turning back on the device that was going to confirm the news that he was over it already. I had no choice. The valet needed to be called to collect my car. How I had missed my beautiful SUV, my cats and only just remembering I have children. Something to look forward to, I suppose, as I gift them the Claddagh rings for each of them.

The message from him comes through straight away with a picture. A yelp in delight followed by a fist pump into the air. I jump onto my friend with the power of a flea leaping from one animal to the next. A picture of his flights booked for next weekend. He was coming to see me.

"I told you I would never let you go. I've got you xxx "

Every weekend now spent travelling back and forth between Ireland and him to the UK. I have finally found a man that meets my needs emotionally and physically. A genuine relationship based on mutual respect and love for each other.

So yes, I have found love. Not in Tinder, but it took Tinder to get me there. Letting me know what my standards are and what I needed to find within myself. No longer will I have to put up with an array of men who use online dating as a sex line and free prostitution. Love finds you in the most unexpected places, and it has certainly found me.

Mr Way Too Young says...

I moved to Ireland two years ago, with a pressure of being wanted by the police. My mother insistent that I run for the stupidity of my crime. One drunken night and my life changed forever. Out on a date with my girl as an inebriated man attempting to touch her inappropriately approached her. I will always protect my woman to the ends of the world. Punching him in the face, landing on the ground harder than I expected. The local news the next morning told of a man who had been assaulted in the street for no reason and the police were looking to speak to a man caught on the CCTV. Now left with no other option but to leave. The absence of my father from a young age showed me the mistakes I should not make. How to treat a woman and make her feel secure. Memories of my mother crying at the kitchen table many nights, worrying about how to pay the bills, struggling to raise me and my sister. I tried to help where I could, but I didn't have a good job with a limited education. I sold drugs, which brought in enough money for her to buy her home.

She would always be stable in her life, never have to feel the fear of not paying the rent at the end of the month. It's not ideal, and I wished there was another way. I knew I had to leave and find a new life for myself.

A Polish community well established in Galway. That is where we decided I should go. I got a job and a room in a house from searching for a Facebook group designed for Poles wishing to emigrate. I settled in quickly, a home from home with enough familiarity of the language and its strange accent. The girls of Ireland are beautiful, with the freedom not allowed with our women. They knew what they wanted and were more liberated than back home. For the next two years, I enjoyed the pleasure of many of them, attracted to my Polish accent and humour. My best mate, my wingman and we often pulled together until one day he came home with news.

"I've been seeing someone for a while. I can't go out with you shagging random females anymore. I've asked her to marry me, and I want you to be the best man."

"Why would you want to do something that stupid? We are men and should enjoy our lives. No commitments. We agreed."

"When you meet someone special, you will change your mind. You'll see. One day a woman will walk into your life, and you will feel as though it has delivered her to you by the angels."
"That will never happen to me. I will not allow it. No-one will win me over."
I am adamant that I will never be in a relationship. The pickings on this island are too fine. Lots to enjoy and sample. Full of intention to get through as many of them as possible. It's hard not to fall back into old ways. The drug dealing business pulled me back by bumping into old contacts that had also made their way here. I had a job in a local factory, invested heavily in crypto currency, so it was just a temporary measure to get money in while I adjusted to this life.
The morning of his wedding has arrived. Even though I agreed to be the best man, I was not happy about this situation. She was going to take him away from me. I would never see him again. That's what wives do: they take control of the husband and rule his life. It lay the rules she had already set down to possess him. I know we were in a catholic country, but was it really that she wouldn't allow him to have sex with her? If you are going to buy into a life of purgatory and misery, then should at least sample

the goods. Here I stand next to him, allowing him to voluntarily enter his life sentence.

The celebration is in full swing, friends and family dancing to the cheesy wedding singer, too drunk to care. No strangers within this eastern European reunion. At the bar I see her, my target for the evening. She doesn't look familiar. Maybe she is related to the bride. As I try to take another look, she has disappeared. I must find her. Full of coke and bravado. I know I can get her into my bed tonight. Not a problem. Call me arrogant or cocksure. I don't care. It's guaranteed with a zero per cent failure rate. Venturing outside, I see her on a bench, cigarette in between her beautiful lips, searching for a lighter she obviously doesn't have. Now is my chance. I can approach her with help and no chat up lines. One flick to produce the flame, lighting up her features, big dark brown eyes, almost black, stare up at me with amusement as she inhales deeply to draw in the nicotine hit. All I can imagine is my cock in her mouth and swilling her throat with my come.

"Thankyou. You rescued me."

"Cześć. Zapraszamy. Are you English?"

"Yes, I am here for a holiday. Not sure on where to go and what to see. Any ideas?"

"I can show you around if you would like that. I have been in Ireland for two years. I know my way round."

Not sure what was happening, felt an unusual jolt in my chest as I looked at her. Is this what my now married friend meant when he said a woman would appear in my life and everything would change? She was older than me, but not by much. Probably had her shit together, unlike most of the girls I usually pick up. There was something so alluring about her, determined to not let her escape from my clutches. My focus was completely on her. Abandoning the wedding party to sit in the hotel bar with her and the best friend. Wishing that she would leave us alone, knowing that I would have to persevere with the company of until she was ready to detach from her security blanket. Her humour was sharp and brutal, not caring how it landed or even if it hurt, like my own. I've never met a woman like this, with no fear of what I said without reprisal or judgement. Could take anything I said to her in my clumsy translations to speak English speaking. I have offended several women since I moved to Ireland unintentionally. It's nice to see she has got her shit together and just brushes it off or laughs loudly. Her authenticity was a welcome surprise and wholly accepted. She pulls herself closer to me, snuggling into my body with her hand on my me. I can feel my hard on begging to be released and enter her as I grab her face and kiss her will all the passion and wanting that I can muster. She must know how much I need her right now. I could happily fuck her over the table in this bar, unconcerned to the other patrons enjoying their drinks.

Every time I try to pull her closer, she resists, "Why are you trying to escape me? You are mine now!"

"I am too old for you by at least twenty years. You are coming to the age when you want to settle down. I'm fifty. Why on earth would you be interested in an old woman?"

Sliding back on the bench, looking at her with wonderment and shock.

"I thought you were only a couple of years older than me. It doesn't bother me. I am comparing you to other women that I have met tonight, and I realise they are just girls. As soon as I saw you, I knew you were the one that I want!"

Quick stop at the all-night shop to stock up on the condoms with a mission to deplete the package of its contents. We arrive at my home. The taxi pulls away as the realisation of two things comes to mind. My room is an absolute mess, as I always go to the girls' home and never invite them over into my world and second, my keys remain on a table somewhere at the hotel. I left the window for my bedroom open. Only one option available to us is to climb. She is dressed for it in her hoody and jeans. That is another strange fact. Usually I am attracted to groomed glamourous girls with big tits and blonde hair. The total opposite stands in front of me with a mass of curls like I have never seen before, no make-up and in casual attire. I push her up the drainpipe using the opportunity to grab her fine arse, with her impressing me with strength to pull herself the rest of the way through the window. She leans out, holding out her hand to help me through as I land on top of her. One look into each other's eyes, the clothes are being ripped off. Uncaring about the damage caused to my shirt as the buttons fly off across the room. She is manically pulling at my belt to release my cock. I plunge my fingers into her pussy, rubbing her magic button inside while flicking the clit. Much to my amazement, she has a powerful orgasm within minutes, spraying me with her juices. I need to taste her nectar flowing into my throat. I am so horny and turned on by her. Never has a woman responded to me in this way.

"Pieprz mnie!"

For a moment I stop, looking at her, stunned.

"You speak Polish?"

"At little, but only the most important words. Not sure of the correct masculine and feminine words. So, as I said before, Fuck me, Proszę!"

"Z przyjemnością"

"The pleasure is all mine. Now come here and stop talking."

There was no need to ask me twice. My cock rammed into her with no guidance. The satisfaction of joining with her was apparent by the loud groans we both release. Banging her with an intensity I never thought possible, all the while keeping contact with her eyes. I can feel the sweat on our bodies mixing with our fluids. Coming together with such power, I don't want to disembark from this ride. Her skin feels clammy beneath my touch, as I feel the palpitations in my heart. I collapse on her, the room spinning, bringing a sickness to my stomach. My chest tightens in pain.

"I can't breathe."

Panic-stricken, she jumps up, stares at me for a brief moment as I take in the full beauty of her naked body, unable to do anything about it. My eyes pleading for her to help me. Why has she left me alone? I'm dying here and she has gone. I can hear voices in the distance as she speaks to my housemate. What must he be thinking? A naked woman running around his house looking for a wet towel. Faintly I can hear her say, "I think I've killed him." Bit dramatic, but could be true. The towel she brings back and throws over me to cool down the fever is not damp, it's wringing wet, extremely cold and doing nothing to make me feel better.

"I think I have taken too much cocaine."

"Are you fucking kidding me? How did you get a hard on?"

How can she question my ability to fuck at a time like this? Although she is right, when on the coke I can't get it up for anyone usually. Another sign telling me she is different. The universe is speaking to me at full volume. Even in my distress, she is making jokes about me, while handing me a lit spliff. I think I am in love! Deeply inhaling the luxurious feel of purple haze skunk, while she settles next to me with her head on her chest. I watch her as she falls asleep, content.

The next morning, I wake up with a raging hard on as I feel the softness of her curves next to me. Turning her to me with gentle kisses, we spend the rest of the morning making love. The first time I have called it this. It feels so different with her, with an overwhelming never to let go of her. I don't know if she is thinking the same way as me or this is just a fling while on holiday. Going back home never to think of me again, the thought was incredibly distressing. I must take advantage of her time here, so I make a quick decision to move into the hotel for the last days with her.

During the day, there are three of us, taking in the delights and sights of the West Atlantic coast road. I show her my favourite beach and revel in her enjoyment of the golden sands and crystal-clear waters. The nights spent alone together, making love alongside pure raw sex, teaching me skills and positions I have heard about, but never believed they were possible. This woman excites in ways I could never have imagined. As each day goes by, the harder it is going to become to wave her goodbye and out of my life.

The day for her to leave has arrived. The sadness felt inside me, wishing she would abandon her life in the UK and stay here with me. I would get us a house, work hard to support her until she was settled.

"We will see each other again. The angels have brought you to me. This is meant to be. Zegnaj na razie piękna."

One last kiss before she climbed in the car.

"Do widzenia" Still impressed that she speaks some Polish, that last goodbye full of sorrow.

I watch her drive away as I decide. Before she has even turned the corner, I am searching for flights. All booked for next weekend in the hope she needs me on the same level. A picture to confirm my feelings for her sent with

"I told you I would never let you go. I've got you xxx "

Every weekend we visit each other with our feeling for each other growing stronger with each visit. I don't care about her age; she is the only woman that I want, and she will be mine forever.

Maria R Peter

About the Author

Liverpool born. Manchester bred gives Maria a unique form of wit. Often dry and very blunt. She grew up in the seventies with a working-class family and often saw the harsh side of life made easier with humour.

She took every opportunity in life that came her way leading her to many different characters across the globe. Being a mother of three and after a successful career in the music industry, she decided to take a step back and convert those personalities into books.

Throughout life, she has always been the funnier one in her social circles, as she often speaks before she thinks, creating situations most of us wouldn't want to be in. Her ethos is bad behaviour makes life more interesting!

Misdemeanoursoftinder.com

Follow on Instagram and Facebook for bonus posts!

Printed in Great Britain
by Amazon

81082345R00133